The Christmas market stalls looked very festive, with strings of brightly coloured lights hanging from their awnings. When they came to a stall that ~~was selling mulled wine. I~~

~~...~~istmas
~~...~~ my sister a~~...~~ ~~...~~eave a glass for Santa to go with his mince pie.'

'And did he drink it?' Max asked, loving the way her eyes had lit up at the memory.

'Of course—or at least somebody did.'

Max laughed. 'Well, you can't *prove* that Father Christmas doesn't exist, can you?'

She shook her head. 'You are completely mad. Do you know that?'

Max felt his breath catch when she smiled up at him. Bending, he placed his mouth over hers. Her lips were cool from the night air, yet he could sense the heat beneath the chill and groaned. Kissing Lucy was like nothing he had ever experienced before!

He drew back reluctantly, seeing the shock in her eyes, and knew that she was as stunned by what had happened as he was.

'I suppose I should apologise, although I'm not sorry that I kissed you,' he said truthfully. Reaching out, he brushed his fingertips over her lips and felt her shudder. T~~...~~ ~~...~~ his voice whe~~...~~ ~~...~~about you~~...~~ ~~...~~ how craz~~...~~

Dear Reader

I always love writing Christmas stories—mainly because I love Christmas. I spend hours shopping for presents for my family, and enjoy every second. I love wrapping the gifts when I get home, and piling them under the tree. I even enjoy visiting the supermarket and buying all the food! But most of all I love the fact that the reason for all the hustle and bustle is because we are celebrating the birth of a child. That's why I decided to set this book in the maternity unit of Dalverston General Hospital.

Consultant Max Curtis and midwife Lucy Harris have both been badly hurt in the past, and they are very wary about getting hurt again. However, as they work together, helping to deliver babies, they soon realise that they are deeply attracted to one another. Neither wants to admit how they feel. It takes a little Christmas magic to make them see that they don't need to be afraid of falling in love.

I wish you all a happy and joyous Christmas, wherever you are.

Jennifer

THE MIDWIFE'S CHRISTMAS MIRACLE

BY
JENNIFER TAYLOR

First published in Great Britain 2010
Harlequin Mills & Boon Limited,
Eton House, 18-24 Paradise Road, Richmond, Surrey TW9 1SR

© Jennifer Taylor 2010

ISBN: 978 0 263 87934 6

Printed and bound in Spain
by Litografia Rosés, S.A., Barcelona

Jennifer Taylor lives in the north-west of England, in a small village surrounded by some really beautiful countryside. She has written for several different Mills & Boon® series in the past, but it wasn't until she read her first Medical™ Romance that she truly found her niche. She was so captivated by these heart-warming stories that she set out to write them herself! When she's not writing, or doing research for her latest book, Jennifer's hobbies include reading, gardening, travel, and chatting to friends both on and off-line. She is always delighted to hear from readers, so do visit her website at www.jennifer-taylor.com

Recent titles by the same author:

THE DOCTOR'S BABY BOMBSHELL*
THE GP'S MEANT-TO-BE BRIDE*
MARRYING THE RUNAWAY BRIDE*
THE SURGEON'S FATHERHOOD SURPRISE**

Dalverston Weddings
**Brides of Penhally Bay*

For my granddaughter, Isobel.
My little ray of sunshine.

CHAPTER ONE

'AND last but definitely not least, this is Max Curtis, our acting consultant. Max, this is Lucy Harris, the new midwife who started today.'

'Nice to meet you, Lucy.'

'You too, Dr…er…er…' Lucy flushed when she realised that she hadn't caught his surname. It was hard to disguise her embarrassment when the dark-haired man seated behind the desk laughed.

'It's Curtis, although most people round here call me Max.' He smiled up at her. 'I'm not picky, mind. "Hey *you*" will get my attention fast enough.'

'That's good to know.' Lucy smiled back, relieved by the easy way he had accepted her gaffe. Obviously, Max Curtis wasn't the type of person who took himself too seriously, unlike some of the consultants she had worked with. 'Although I promise that I won't forget your name from now on. I won't dare!'

He chuckled softly, his dark brown eyes creasing at the corners. 'Don't worry about it. The first day in a new job is always a nightmare. There's so much to take in that you don't know if you're on your head or your heels most of the time.'

'That's true,' Lucy agreed. 'I just hope everyone

will be as understanding as you when I get their names muddled up!'

'They will be,' he assured her then reached for the phone when it started to ring. 'Maternity. Max Curtis speaking.'

Lucy sighed as she moved away from the desk, hoping that would be the end of the introductory tour. She honestly didn't think that she could cope with having to remember anyone else. Joanna, the young trainee midwife who had been delegated to show her around, grinned at her.

'That's it. You've met everyone now, apart from the staff who are working tonight and Anna Kearney, our consultant. She's on maternity leave at the moment, so you have that pleasure to come.'

'At least that's one less name to forget,' Lucy declared, rolling her eyes.

'As Max said, nobody will worry about it,' Joanna assured her. She led the way along the corridor, pausing outside the door to one of the delivery suites. There were four suites in total and Lucy knew that every one was currently occupied. Although the maternity unit at Dalverston General was smaller than the one she had worked on in Manchester, she had a feeling that it wasn't going to be any less busy because of that.

'Margaret's going off duty soon and Amanda wants you to take over from her,' Joanna explained, passing on the instructions the senior midwife had given her. 'I've got to help sort out the breakfasts now so I'll have to leave you here. Is that OK?'

'Fine,' Lucy assured her. She smoothed down her brand-new uniform top as Joanna hurried away then tapped on the door and went in, smiling at the middle-aged woman standing beside the bed. 'I believe I'm taking over from you.'

'That's right.' Margaret returned her smile. 'We were hoping that Sophie's baby would arrive while I was still on duty but he's proving to be a tad reluctant to make his appearance in the world.'

'Obviously a determined little chap who knows his own mind,' Lucy said lightly. She went over to the bed and introduced herself to the young mother-to-be. 'Hello, Sophie, my name is Lucy Harris and I've just started working here today. I'll be looking after you when Margaret goes home.'

'You are a proper midwife, though?' Sophie said anxiously. 'You're not just a trainee?'

'No. I've been a midwife for four years and I've delivered lots of babies during that time,' Lucy explained. It wasn't ideal to have to hand over a patient in the middle of a delivery and she was keen to allay the girl's fears. 'I worked at a hospital in Manchester before I came here.'

'Oh, I see. Well, that's all right, I suppose.'

Sophie still sounded a little dubious but Lucy understood. The relationship between a mother and her midwife was a delicate one and needed to be based on trust if it was to be successful. She patted Sophie's hand. 'Everything is going to be fine, Sophie, believe me. Now, if you don't mind, I'd like Margaret to update me as to what progress you've made.'

Sophie closed her eyes as Lucy moved away from the bed. She looked both exhausted and extremely anxious as she settled back against the pillows. Lucy frowned as she studied the girl's strained face.

'When was she admitted?'

'Just before eight p.m. last night,' Margaret replied. 'Her contractions were quite strong, so I was hopeful it would be a fairly speedy delivery even though it's her first baby. Unfortunately, everything started to slow down a couple of hours later and now we've come to a complete standstill.'

'How's the baby doing?' Lucy queried.

'Fine. Heartbeat is strong and there's no signs of distress. It's just going to be one of those stop-go deliveries from the look of it, which is a pity because I was hoping to get it over as quickly as possible.' Margaret must have seen the question in Lucy's eyes and lowered her voice. 'Sophie's not got anyone with her, you see. From what I can gather, the baby's father took off a couple of months ago and she's not seen him since.'

'What about family or friends?' Lucy asked sympathetically.

'She's never mentioned her family so I've no idea what the situation is there. As for friends, well, she hasn't lived in Dalverston all that long. Apparently, the baby's father got a job at the industrial park and that's why they moved here.' Margaret sighed. 'I feel really sorry for her because she's been very much on her own since he disappeared off the scene.'

'What a terrible shame.'

Lucy's heart went out to the girl, although she couldn't help thinking that even if Sophie had had friends and family to support her, it might not have helped. As she knew to her cost, sometimes it was the people you were closest to who let you down most of all.

The thought sent a shaft of pain surging through her but she forced it down. She refused to dwell on the past when she had moved to Dalverston to escape it.

She read through the notes Margaret had made then checked Sophie's pulse and BP, the baby's heartbeat, all the routine tasks that were so essential to the eventual outcome. She had just finished when the door opened and Max Curtis appeared.

'Hi! I thought I'd check to see what progress we're making,' he said as he came over to the bed.

Lucy stepped aside to give him room, somewhat surprised to discover how tall he was. He had been sitting down when they had been introduced so she'd had no idea that he must be at least six feet tall with a leanly muscular physique under a pair of well-cut dark grey trousers and a paler grey shirt. All of a sudden she felt unusually conscious of her own lack of inches. At a mere five feet two, she could best be described as petite, although a lushly feminine figure did make up for what she lacked in height.

'Everything seems to have come to a dead stop, Dr Curtis,' Sophie said forlornly. 'I don't understand why it's happened.'

'It just does sometimes, Sophie,' he assured her. 'It's all systems go and then everything suddenly tails off. Are you still having contractions?'

'No. I've not had one for ages now.'

'Let me take a look and then we'll decide what we're going to do.'

He gently examined her, explaining what he was doing as he checked the position of the baby and how far her cervix had dilated. Lucy appreciated the fact that he didn't rush. He appeared to have all the time in the world and she knew that it would reassure Sophie more than anything else would do. She was pleased to see that the girl looked far less anxious by the time he finished and explained that he was going to give her something to help restart her contractions.

He wrote out an instruction for an intravenous infusion of synthetic oxytocin to be administered. This would augment the naturally occurring oxytocin that caused the muscles in the uterus to contract. He handed it to Lucy after she told him that Margaret was going off duty. 'I'll check back with you later to see what progress we're making. In the meantime, get the switchboard to page me if you have any concerns.'

'I shall,' Lucy concurred.

'Hopefully, this should get things back on track,' he added, slipping his pen back into his pocket. 'We'll give nature a bit of a boost and hope it'll do its stuff.'

'Always the best solution,' she agreed. She had never been an advocate of rushing in unnecessarily and it was good to know that they were in accord in that respect.

'It seems we're in agreement, then.' Max smiled at her then headed towards the door. 'Right, now I'm off to make myself a large cup of black coffee. I need a *serious* injection of caffeine if I'm to get through the rest of the day.'

'That sounds like desperation talking,' Lucy replied lightly.

'Oh, it is, believe me. Given half the chance, I would curl up in this doorway and fall fast asleep!'

He laughed but Lucy could tell that he was only partly joking. She frowned as she took stock of the lines etched either side of his mouth, the weariness in his dark brown eyes, and realised all of a sudden how exhausted he looked.

'Didn't you get much sleep last night?'

'I didn't get any. I was about to get into bed when

I was called back here to see a patient. Eclampsia,' he added succinctly.

'Oh, I see.' Lucy nodded, understanding why he had needed to rush back into work. Eclampsia was a highly dangerous condition for both a mother and her child. It could lead to convulsions and even coma and death if not treated in time. Normally, the condition was picked up as pre-eclampsia during routine antenatal screening. The combination of high blood pressure, protein in the urine and oedema—an accumulation of fluid in the tissues—were all indications of it. She was surprised that alarm bells hadn't started ringing earlier, in fact.

'Was there no sign beforehand that the mother was at risk?' she asked curiously.

'None at all. Mind you, the fact that she missed her last couple of antenatal appointments didn't help.' Max sighed. 'When I asked her why she hadn't been to the clinic, she said that she hadn't had the time. Apparently, she had a hair appointment on the first occasion and needed to get her nails done the next time.'

'Unbelievable!' Lucy exclaimed.

'Yep. I think that just about sums it up. Fortunately, her husband phoned us when she started complaining that she had a headache and that her vision was blurred. He was told to bring her straight in so she was here when she had a convulsion. We administered anti-convulsant drugs and I delivered the baby by Caesarean section. He's in the special care baby unit, but I'm pretty sure he'll be fine. Mum will need monitoring for the next few weeks but she should be all right too.' He shrugged. 'It was worth a sleepless night, all things considered.'

He sketched her a wave and left, his long legs striding along the corridor. Lucy watched him for a moment then closed the door and went to set up the drip. Funnily enough she had enjoyed talking to him. Max Curtis had a relaxed and friendly manner that had put her at her ease, made her feel more positive about the changes she had made to her life recently. Hopefully, moving to Dalverston had been the right thing to do.

She sighed as the doubts suddenly surfaced again. It had been hard to leave her last job when she had been so happy there, harder still to leave all her friends and family behind, but she'd had no choice. Although her parents had tried to persuade her not to go, Lucy knew how difficult it would have been for them if she'd stayed. After all, it wasn't *their* fault that her cousin and her ex-fiancé had had an affair.

Lucy took a deep breath and quelled the moment of panic. She had made her decision and even if it didn't work out as well as she hoped it would, at least it would give her a breathing space, time to put things into perspective. She simply had to remember how much worse it would have been if she'd found out about Richard and Amy *after* the wedding had taken place.

Max made his way to the staffroom then realised that he didn't even have the energy to make himself a cup of coffee. Veering away from the door, he headed for the lift. The cafeteria should be open soon and the thought of a double espresso with his name on it was too tempting to resist.

The staff were just opening up when he arrived, so he gave them his order and sat down, feeling weariness washing over him. The long night had taken its toll, especially as it had been the second night in a row that he'd been called in. With Anna on maternity leave, he had been picking up more than his share of extra hours recently. It wasn't a new occurrence, by any means. Working long and unsocial hours was par for the course in medicine. At one point, he'd been only too glad to work any time he was needed, too. It had been far less stressful dealing with his patients' problems than what had been happening in his marriage.

Max frowned. It was rare that he thought about the past and it surprised him that he should do so now. He had been divorced for three years and he had closed the door on that episode in his life. OK, so he was willing to admit that it had had a knock-on effect, in that he avoided commitment these days, but to his mind that was common sense. Once bitten, twice shy seemed a sensible maxim to live by and he wasn't going to put himself through all that heartache again.

His thoughts moved away from the less than appealing subject of his failed marriage and on to the far more interesting topic of their new midwife. Lucy Harris appeared both highly competent and extremely capable, and he was pleased that their views were in accord. Some of the older midwives were a little entrenched in their ways and it would be good to have a soul-mate on the unit.

The fact that she was also extremely pretty with those huge blue eyes and those shiny auburn curls tumbling around her cheeks was another point in her favour. Although Max shied away from commitment, he had a normal healthy interest in the opposite sex and Lucy Harris was a very attractive member of it. All of sudden his tiredness lifted and he grinned. Working with the lovely Lucy could turn out to be a real tonic.

CHAPTER TWO

SOPHIE JONES'S baby finally made his appearance in the middle of the afternoon. Amanda, the senior midwife, helped Lucy deliver him. Lucy guessed that Amanda was keen to put her through her paces, but tried not to let it worry her. By the time Sophie and baby Alfie were transferred to a ward, she was confident that Amanda wouldn't have any more concerns about her, and it was reassuring to know that at least one very important aspect of her life hadn't changed.

Lucy fetched her coat at the end of her shift and left. It had started raining at lunchtime and the gutters were brimming over with water as she made her way to the bus stop. She huddled against the wall when a car sped past, sending a wave of water across the pavement, but by the time she reached the bus stop, her shoes and trousers were soaked through. She joined the queue, hoping that she wouldn't have to wait too long. However, half an hour later she was still there when a car drew up and Max Curtis poked his head out of the window.

'Do you want a lift?' He glanced at her sodden trousers and grimaced. 'You're going to catch your death if you stand there much longer. Hop in.'

Lucy hesitated, not sure that accepting a lift would

be the right thing to do. It didn't seem fair to expect him
to drive her home after the long day he'd had. However,
the thought of getting out of the rain was too tempting
to resist. She slid into the passenger seat and slammed
the door.

'Thanks. It's really good of you,' she said gratefully.
'I don't know what happened to the bus. I've been waiting ages and there's been no sign of it.'

'Probably two will turn up together,' he said lightly,
putting the car into gear. 'So how was your first day
then? Not too scary, I hope.'

'No, it was fine,' Lucy assured him. 'Everyone was
really helpful, which makes a huge difference when
you're starting a new job.'

'It's a good team,' he assured her, slowing as they
came to a set of traffic lights on red. 'Most of them
have worked on the unit for a while, so that helps, of
course.'

'It must do,' Lucy agreed, turning to look at him.
Although he wasn't classically handsome, he was
certainly attractive, she decided. The combination of
those highly masculine features—a strong jaw, straight
nose and perfectly sculpted lips—was very appealing.
Rumpled dark brown hair falling across his forehead
lent him a rakish air that many women would find pleas-
ing too. She found it strangely engaging which surprised
her, given what had happened recently.

'I'm looking forward to being part of a settled team,'
she said, hurriedly squashing that thought. She certainly
wasn't in the market for another relationship. The fact
that her ex-fiancé had betrayed her had destroyed her
faith in men. Love, marriage and, most important of
all, a family had always been her dream but not any

more. She wouldn't give any man that much power over her again. 'The turnover of staff at my last place was a nightmare. You no sooner got used to working with someone before they left.'

'It's always more of a problem in the city. Staff tend to move around more than they do in rural areas. You were at the Royal, weren't you?' he asked, glancing at her.

'That's right. I was there for almost four years. It was really busy, but I enjoyed working there.'

'So what brought you to Dalverston?' he asked, returning his attention to the road as the lights changed. 'Has your family relocated to this part of the world?'

'No, only me.'

'Really?' He shot her a look and she saw the surprise on his face. 'It takes guts to up sticks and leave everything behind like that.'

'I don't know about that. It just felt like the right thing to do,' she hedged, not wanting to go into detail about the reasons for her decision. She sighed softly. Maybe it was silly to feel embarrassed, but what had happened had dented her confidence. She no longer saw herself as the person she had always been, but as a reject, second best. For some reason she hated to think that Max might see her like that too.

'I realised that I was in a bit of a rut and needed a complete change of scene,' she explained, wondering why it mattered what he thought. She barely knew him, so his opinion wasn't going to make much difference to her. 'When I saw the advert for Dalverston, I decided to apply for the post.'

'And got it.' He gave her a quick smile but Lucy could tell that he'd guessed there was more to the story than she'd admitted. 'Well, the Royal's loss is our gain is all I can say.'

He didn't press her and she was glad about that. Maybe it would get easier with time but at the moment it was still too painful to talk about what had happened. They drove into the town centre and she gave him directions to where she lived from there.

Finding somewhere suitable had been harder than she'd expected. Although rent in Dalverston was less expensive than it was in Manchester, it was still a big chunk out of her monthly salary. She and Richard had signed a lease on their flat and there were still several months left to run. Richard had refused to pay his share of the rent after he'd moved out, and unwilling to make the situation even more unpleasant than it already was, Lucy hadn't tried to persuade him. Instead, she'd been paying it all and had needed to trim her costs accordingly. She'd finally settled on a flat in one of the old terraced houses close to the high street. It wasn't the best location but it would do for now. She would find somewhere better when she could afford it.

Max drew up outside. 'Here you are then. Home sweet home.' He glanced up at the building and frowned. 'It looks a bit grim. Couldn't you find anywhere better than this?'

'It's fine, really.' Lucy reached for the door handle, not wanting to explain why her options had been so limited. 'Thanks again for the lift. I only hope I haven't taken you too far out of your way.'

'Not at all. In fact, it isn't all that far from where I live, funnily enough. I just didn't recognise the name of the road. I don't think I've been down here before.'

'You've not missed much,' Lucy assured him wryly, opening the car door. 'I'll see you tomorrow, I expect.'

'You will.'

He waited while she unlocked the front door then drove away, but it was a moment before she went inside. As she watched the car's taillights disappear around a bend, Lucy felt a wave of loneliness wash over her. All of a sudden the evening stretched before her, all those empty hours to fill. She couldn't help thinking about how her life had used to be, when she had come home from work and Richard had been there.

She sighed because she'd honestly believed they'd been happy. Even when Richard had started making excuses and going out at night, she hadn't suspected a thing. It was only when Amy, stricken with guilt, had confessed that Lucy had discovered what had been going on. The fact that she'd felt like such a fool had made it all the more painful.

She took a deep breath and closed the door. It was all in the past now and she had moved on. Even though she didn't feel like the same person, she would survive and build a new life for herself. Just for a moment a picture of Max Curtis appeared in her mind's eye before she dismissed it. Max might play a small role in her life but no man was going to take centre stage ever again.

Max drove home thinking about what Lucy had told him or, rather, what she hadn't said. He'd seen the sadness in her eyes and suspected there was more to her decision to relocate than she had admitted. Had she broken up with her partner, perhaps? If that was the case, then it must have been a very painful split if she'd felt the need to leave everything behind.

He sighed as he turned into the car park of the modern apartment block where he lived. He knew only too well how it felt to want to escape. He'd done that himself, hadn't he? After his marriage had ended, he'd left London and come north, seeking a fresh start. Although he couldn't change the fact that his life was never going to turn out how he'd expected it would, it had helped to meet new people and form new friendships.

Nowadays he was far more philosophical. So what if he could never father a child? It was a blow, yes, but he had come to terms with the idea now and accepted it. At least he knew the truth so there was no danger of him ruining any other woman's life.

Marriage was off the agenda for obvious reasons and any relationships he had were strictly for fun. Maybe it wasn't the life he'd once envisaged for himself, but he couldn't complain. He had a job he loved, good friends and enough money to buy whatever he wanted. In fact, he couldn't understand why he was even thinking about it. Had Lucy Harris been the trigger? But why? What was it about her that made him suddenly wish he could change things?

He had no idea but it was something he needed to bear in mind. Lovely though Lucy was, he didn't intend to get his fingers burned a second time.

Lucy was rostered to work at the antenatal clinic the following morning. She went straight there after she'd signed in and the first person she saw was Max. He was chatting to the receptionist, laughing at something the girl was saying. He looked so relaxed that she felt her spirits immediately lift. It had been a long night and she'd had difficulty sleeping, but there was something about Max that made her feel much more positive about life.

He glanced round when he heard her footsteps and grinned at her. 'Ahah! I see you've drawn the short straw, Lucy. We'll be working together this morning. Is that OK with you?'

'Fine.' She returned his smile, wondering why he had this effect on her. It wasn't anything he said, more a feeling he exuded, and it was very welcome too. 'I've no problem with that.'

'Good.' He gave her a warm smile as he led the way to the consulting room and sat down at the desk while he brought up the list of appointments on the computer. 'It's rather a mixed bag this morning. Normally, we try to split the list so that one of us sees the mums who are here for their first visits while the other deals with the rest. Unfortunately, we're short-staffed today because Diane is off sick. It means you won't have as much time with the new mums as you'd probably like.'

'I'll make up for it at a later date. Most women are a little anxious when they come for their first visit to the clinic and they find it difficult to take everything in. It's usually better to talk to them and discuss their options at their second or third appointment, I find.'

'That's great. I'm glad it isn't going to cause you a problem.' He turned his attention back to the screen, scrolling through the list of names until he came to the one he wanted. 'This is a case I'd like you to be involved in. Mum's name is Helen Roberts. It's her first baby and she had pre-existing diabetes mellitus when she got pregnant.'

'How has she been?' Lucy asked, walking around the desk. She bent down so she could see the screen, feeling her nostrils tingle as she inhaled the citrus-fresh tang of the shampoo he'd used. She couldn't help comparing it to the rather cloying scent of the one Richard had preferred.

'Extremely well so far. We run a pre-pregnancy clinic at Dalverston for women with established diabetes. It's a joint venture between us and the diabetes care team and our main aim is to ensure that blood glucose levels are under control before and at the time of conception.'

'There's a slightly increased risk of the baby being malformed if the blood glucose level isn't right, isn't there?' Lucy questioned, straightening up. She moved back to the other side of the desk, unsure why it troubled her to make the comparison. What difference did it make if she preferred the smell of Max's shampoo?

'There is, which is why a woman with diabetes should seek advice *before* she gets pregnant. As I expect you know, there are increased risks for the mother as well as for the baby. Retinopathy can be a problem for anyone who has diabetes, as can high blood pressure, but there's more chance of them becoming an issue when a woman is pregnant. And of course there's a greater risk of mum suffering from pre-eclampsia, too.'

'It must be daunting for a woman to be faced with all that,' Lucy said quickly, determined to nip such foolishness in the bud by focusing on their patient.

Max shrugged. 'It must be. Thankfully, Helen is a very level-headed sort of person. She's a farmer's wife and has a very practical approach to life. She understood the risks from the outset and has coped extremely well. We've been working closely with the diabetes care team and she's undergone all the recommended tests and assessments.'

'How about the baby?' Lucy asked. 'Is it much larger than normal?'

'Slightly larger than would be expected at this stage but not worryingly so.'

'Controlling the blood glucose level is key, isn't it? If the level isn't strictly controlled, there may be an increase in the amount of glucose that reaches the baby so that it grows faster than normal.'

'Either that or its growth may be stunted,' Max explained. 'I've seen several cases like that and there were complications each time following the births.'

'How many weeks is she?' Lucy asked.

'Thirty-two,' he replied promptly, not needing to refer to his notes.

It was clear from that how interested he was in the case and she couldn't help admiring the fact that it was obviously more than just a job to him. She'd noticed that yesterday, too, when he'd examined Sophie. His patience and refusal to rush were indications of a genuine concern for his patients. She'd worked with a lot of doctors and, sadly, some had treated the mums-to-be in a very cavalier fashion. It was good to know that Max wasn't of that ilk.

'As you know, it's even more important to control blood glucose levels towards the end of the pregnancy.' He picked up a slip of paper and handed it to her. 'Helen has been attending the diabetes clinic on a weekly basis recently. She was there yesterday and the registrar was concerned because her glucose levels have started fluctuating. That's why we're seeing her today. We may need to arrange for her to have another ultrasound to check the amniotic fluid volume as well as the baby's growth.'

Lucy quickly read the note. She sighed as she handed it back to him. 'What a shame that it should happen now after she's been doing so well.'

'Isn't it?' He grimaced. 'Knowing Helen, she will blame herself for this and that's where you can help, Lucy. I want you to make her understand that it isn't anything she's done wrong. The last thing we want is her getting stressed. It won't help her or the baby.'

'Of course. I'll do anything I can,' she assured him.

'Thanks.'

He gave her a quick smile and she felt a trickle of warmth flow through her when she saw the approval it held. Once again, she felt her spirits lift and it was such an odd feeling when her mood had been so down-beat recently. She wasn't sure why Max had this effect on her and didn't have a chance to work it out as he continued.

'Right, now that's sorted out we'd better make a start or we'll still be here at midnight.'

Lucy went to the door and called in their first patient. She'd always enjoyed meeting the mums and being involved in their care and she realised that she was looking forward to it more than ever that day. Knowing that she was part of a team that really cared about these women and their babies made the job so worthwhile.

All of a sudden she was glad that she had made the move to Dalverston, and not just because she'd escaped from a difficult situation either. She would learn a lot from working here, learn a lot from working with Max, too. For the first time in ages, it felt as though she had something to look forward to.

CHAPTER THREE

'Lucy will have a word with you on your next visit, Rachel. You'll be able to decide what you want to do then. Isn't that right, Lucy?'

Max sat back in his seat while Lucy took over. They made a good team, he thought, listening as she explained how they would work out a birth plan the next time Rachel came to the clinic, before she escorted her out to Reception. Although her predecessor had been an excellent midwife, she'd been a little brusque at times. He knew that some of the younger women in particular had found her intimidating, but that definitely wasn't the case with Lucy. She had a gently reassuring manner that put even the most nervous mums at their ease. He couldn't remember when he'd last enjoyed a clinic so much, in fact.

He was in the process of absorbing that thought when she came back into the room. His brows lifted when he saw the frown on her face. 'Is something wrong?'

'I'm not sure. Apparently, Helen Roberts hasn't turned up. From what you told me, it seems rather strange that she would miss an appointment, doesn't it?'

'It's not like Helen,' he agreed. He brought up Helen's file on the computer and checked her phone number. 'I'll give her a call and see what's happened to her.'

He picked up the phone then stopped when his pager suddenly bleeped. It was the code for the maternity unit, so he dialled their number first. 'It's Max. You paged me.' His heart sank when Amanda informed him that Helen Roberts had just been admitted. 'I'll be right there.'

'Problems?' Lucy asked as he hastily stood up.

'Helen Roberts has been rushed in by ambulance. It appears she collapsed on the bus on her way here.'

'That explains why she didn't keep her appointment!' Lucy exclaimed. 'Are you going up to Maternity to see her?'

'Yes.' Max picked up his jacket off the back of the chair and shrugged it on. 'The diabetes care team will need to know what's happened. Can you give them a call for me, please? I've been liaising with Adam Sanders, their registrar, so can you see if he's available? I'd really like his input.'

'Of course.'

Lucy reached for the receiver at the same moment as he went to pass it to her and he felt a ripple of awareness shoot through him when their hands brushed, and quickly drew back. He cleared his throat, unsure why it had happened.

'I'll leave you to sort it out, then. Can you phone Amanda and let her know if Adam can make it? He knows Helen and it will be easier if he reviews the case rather than bring someone else up to speed.'

'Will do.'

'Thanks.' Max turned away, wondering if he'd imagined the faintly breathy note in her voice. Had that brief moment of contact affected her as much as it had affected him?

He sighed as he made his way to the lift because it was stupid to think that Lucy had even noticed what had happened. It had been the briefest touch, after all, and he had no idea why he was making such a big deal of it. It certainly wasn't like him to behave this way.

Although he appreciated the power of sexual attraction, these days sex was merely a means to satisfy a need. There was never an emotional connection between him and the women he slept with. It had never worried him before because that was exactly what he had wanted: to remain detached. However, all of a sudden he found himself wishing for more. How good it must feel to make love to a woman and know that he was the centre of her universe.

Lucy made arrangements for the diabetes registrar to visit the maternity unit then phoned Amanda to let her know he was on his way. She offered to go back and help, but Amanda assured her they could manage and told her to go for lunch. They had a mum booked in to be induced that afternoon and she needed Lucy there.

Lucy tidied up then made her way to the staff canteen. The place was packed when she arrived but she spotted Joanna sitting at a table in the corner with a couple of her friends. Once she had paid for her lunch, she went to join them.

'Do you mind if I sit here?'

'Of course not!' Joanna grinned at her. 'So how did you get on at clinic? I bet it was busy with Diane being off sick.'

'It was.' Lucy sat down and started to peel the plastic film off her tuna mayo sandwich. 'Max was brilliant, though. Even though the list was horrendous he made everyone feel as though he had all the time in the world for them.'

'Uh-oh! It sounds as though we've added another member to the Max Curtis fan club,' Joanna declared, laughing.

'Of course not!' Lucy blushed. She hadn't realised that she'd sounded quite so enthusiastic and hurried to explain. 'It's just nice to work with someone who obviously cares so much about his patients.'

'Ah, so that's it, is it? You admire Max's qualities as a doctor, nothing else?'

'Of course not,' Lucy stated firmly, trying to ignore the niggling little voice that was whispering it wasn't true. Had she imagined that brief moment of awareness that had passed between them? she wondered uneasily. It had been over and done with in a nanosecond so it was hard to believe that it hadn't been her imagination playing tricks.

'I'm not interested in Max, if that's what you think,' she reiterated, as much for her own benefit as anyone else's. She must have sounded convincing because Joanna shrugged.

'Fair enough. It's probably a good thing, too. At least you won't end up disappointed.'

'What do you mean?' Lucy asked in surprise. 'Why should I be disappointed?'

'Oh, just that there's no point setting your sights on Max, is there, girls?' Joanna glanced at the other women who shook their heads. 'You see, Lucy, dishy though Max is, he has one major flaw—he doesn't do commitment. He's quite up-front about it, mind you, makes no bones about the fact that love and marriage aren't on his agenda, so that's something in his favour. A lot of men string a woman along but at least whoever Max goes out with knows the score.'

The conversation moved on to something else but Lucy found it hard to concentrate. What Joanna had told her simply didn't gel with what she had seen. Max didn't seem like the type of man who moved from woman to woman in pursuit of personal pleasure. He cared too much about people to enjoy that kind of life in her opinion, although maybe she wasn't the best person to judge. After what had happened with Richard, she couldn't claim to be an expert on men, could she?

A familiar ache filled her heart but for some reason it didn't seem as painful as it used to be. If she was honest, the thought of Max living the life of an eternal bachelor hurt far more. Maybe it was silly but she felt let down and it was worrying to know that she had made another mistake. From now on she must see Max for what he was: just another man who was out for all he could get.

'Thanks for coming.'

Max shook Adam Sanders's hand then went back into the side room. Helen Roberts had suffered a hypoglycaemic attack after her blood glucose levels had dropped too low. Although she was stable now, it was a blow after she had done so well. He could see the worry in her eyes when he went over to the bed.

'It was just a blip, Helen. You heard what Dr Sanders said, that you've been doing too much and need to rest more. So long as you follow his advice, there's no reason why it should happen again.'

'I was only trying to get everything ready for when the baby arrives,' Helen protested. 'Martin broke his leg last week. One of the bullocks barged into him when he went to feed them, so he's out of action at the moment. I thought I'd finish setting up the nursery—put up the cot and unpack all the baby clothes, things like that. I wasn't doing anything more than any other mum would do.'

'But you aren't just any other mum,' Max reminded her gently. 'All that extra work knocked your glucose levels out of kilter. Add to that the growing demands of the baby, combined with the tendency for insulin resistance to increase during pregnancy and you have a recipe for disaster.'

'I know you're right, Dr Curtis, but it's so hard. I want to do what other women do and get ready for when my baby arrives.' Tears began to trickle down her cheeks and he patted her hand comfortingly.

'I understand that, Helen. But you've got this far and it seems silly to take any risks. Why not let your husband do the unpacking? He's probably sick of being laid up with nothing to do and will enjoy it.'

'Heaven knows what state the place will be in after he's finished!' Helen declared. 'Martin isn't exactly the tidiest of men.'

'I'm sure he'll make a special effort if you ask him.'

'You're right. He will.' Helen wiped her eyes and smiled. 'He's just so thrilled about this baby. We thought we might not be able to have a family because of my diabetes, you see, so it's like a dream come true.'

'It must be.'

Max dredged up a smile but the comment had struck a chord. He had always loved children and had assumed that he would have some of his own one day. Both his brothers had kids and he'd had no reason to think that he would be any different to them. Finding out that the chances of him ever fathering a child were virtually nil had rocked his whole world. Although he'd thought he had accepted it, he suddenly found himself thinking how marvellous it would be if a miracle happened….

He cut off that thought. He wasn't going to put himself through all the heartache of wishing for the impossible to happen. 'I'd like to keep you in overnight, Helen. Dr Sanders wants to monitor your blood glucose levels for the next twenty-four hours and I'd feel happier if you were here while it's done.'

'I understand, Dr Curtis.' Helen sounded resigned. 'Best to be safe rather than sorry.'

'It's just a precaution,' he assured her. 'I'll pop back later to check on you. In the meantime, you're to lie there and rest.'

Max made his way to the desk. Amanda was talking to Lucy when he arrived and he smiled when they both looked up. 'Sorry to interrupt, but I wanted you to know that I'm keeping Helen Roberts in overnight. I know it means tying up the side room but I'd feel happier if she was here while everything settles down. One of the diabetes care team will be popping in at intervals to check her blood glucose levels.'

'That's fine,' Amanda assured him. 'In fact, it will be the perfect opportunity for Lucy to meet her. I know Helen was concerned when Maria left. She was worried in case her replacement didn't have any experience of diabetic pregnancies. You can set her mind at rest, can't you, Lucy?'

'Of course.'

'If there's anything you aren't sure about, I'd be happy

to run through it with you,' Max offered, but Lucy shook her head.

'That won't be necessary, thank you. I've worked with a number of women who had diabetes and I understand the problems they can face during the birth.'

Her tone was so cool that Max frowned. He had the distinct impression that he had upset her, although for the life of him he couldn't think what he'd done. When she excused herself, he went to follow her then stopped when Amanda asked him about the patient they were inducing that afternoon. By the time they had sorted everything out, Lucy had disappeared.

Max was sorely tempted to track her down but in the end he decided not to bother. What could he say to her, anyway? That he was sorry for committing some unknown misdemeanour?

He sighed as he headed to the canteen for a late lunch. Lucy Harris might be a very attractive woman, but that was as far as it went. He had worked out a life-plan for himself and he had no intention of ditching it just because he suddenly found himself harbouring all these crazy ideas.

Maybe Lucy was the type of woman who'd been *born* to have kids, but that had nothing to do with him. The truth was that he was no use to Lucy or any other woman in that respect.

Lucy spent a productive half-hour with Helen Roberts. They discussed Helen's birth plan and Lucy was pleased to see that although Helen hoped for a normal vaginal birth, she was realistic enough to know it might not be possible. By the time Helen's husband, Martin, arrived, she felt they had established a genuine rapport.

'You've been really great,' Helen enthused as she gathered up her notes. 'Maria was very nice but she could be a little intimidating at times, couldn't she, Martin?'

'She certainly put the wind up me,' Martin replied drolly. 'Put it this way, I wouldn't have crossed her!'

'So long as you're happy, that's the main thing,' Lucy said, not wanting to be drawn into a discussion about her predecessor. It would be highly unprofessional for one thing and very unfair when she had never met the woman. 'Now, don't forget that if you're at all worried then you can always phone me. If I'm tied up then leave a message and I'll call you back.'

'Thank you. I really appreciate that. You've been so kind, just like Dr Curtis has,' Helen declared. 'He's really lovely, isn't he? I can't believe that nobody has snapped him up but one of the other mums told me that he isn't married. Is he seeing anyone, do you know?'

'I've no idea.' Lucy summoned a smile, trying to ignore the hollow ache inside her. She wasn't sure why she found the idea of Max's playboy lifestyle so upsetting but she did. 'I've only been here for a couple of days so I haven't had time to get up to speed with the gossip.'

'Well, make sure you do.' Helen grinned at her. 'I don't know what your situation is, Lucy, but you and Dr Curtis would make a lovely couple, if you want my opinion.'

'Which she doesn't.' Martin shook his head when Lucy blushed. 'Now see what you've done, Helen. You've embarrassed her.'

'Rubbish!' Helen said stoutly. 'It was only a bit of fun. You're not embarrassed, are you, Lucy?'

'Of course not,' Lucy lied, wishing the floor would open up and swallow her. She said goodbye and left, but as she made her way to the office she couldn't help thinking about what Helen had said. If the circumstances had been different, would she have seen Max as a potential partner?

Her heart sank because she knew it was true. On the surface, at least, Max was just the kind of man she'd always found attractive. It wasn't just how he looked either. His relaxed and easygoing manner didn't detract from the fact that he was deeply committed to the welfare of his patients, and that was a definite turn-on. That he didn't pull rank and treated the nursing staff as equals was another point in his favour. It was his private life she had an issue with, and that really and truly wasn't any of her business.

Lucy took a deep breath. What Max did in his free time was up to him.

CHAPTER FOUR

THE week rolled to an end and Max had the weekend off for once. He spent it at his brother Simon's house in Leeds. With three boisterous children under the age of ten, it was non-stop chaos from morning till night, but he enjoyed every minute. Being part of a family was a joy, even though it did leave him feeling secretly downhearted about his own life. Although he had a great job and some wonderful friends, it wasn't the same. He couldn't help envying his brother his good fortune.

He drove back to Dalverston early on the Monday morning and went straight to work. When he arrived, everyone was gathered in the staffroom for the monthly team meeting so he poured himself a cup of coffee and went to join them. The meetings had been his idea. Although they were informal affairs, they gave the staff an opportunity to raise any concerns they had. He found it invaluable to be able to discuss any issues before they turned into major problems.

'Morning, everyone.' He took his seat and glanced around the room. Diane was back from sick leave, looking a little peaky, but obviously feeling better. 'Good to have you back,' he said before his gaze moved on. His heart squeezed in an extra beat when he spotted Lucy sitting in the corner. Although he had seen her only briefly in passing since she had refused his offer of help, he had found himself thinking about her frequently, especially over the weekend. As he'd played with his nieces and nephew, he had kept imagining how well she would have fitted in and it was worrying to know that he was thinking along those lines.

Since his divorce, he had kept his personal life in strictly defined compartments: one for his parents and brothers, and another for the women who made brief appearances on the scene. He had never, ever, mixed the two, yet for some reason he had found himself wishing that he could introduce Lucy to his family.

'Good morning,' he said with a smile that would hopefully disguise how alarmed he felt. What was it about her that made him want to break all his rules? He wished he knew because maybe then he would be able to do something about it.

'Good morning,' she replied politely.

Max frowned when he heard the cool note in her voice. Once again he was left with the impression that he was *persona non grata* and it was very strange. What had he done to offend her, he wondered, and how could he make amends? And why in heaven's name did it matter so much?

There was no time to dwell on it right then, however. By necessity the meetings needed to be brief and there was a lot to cover. They discussed various matters but the issue that concerned everyone most of all was the difficulty they were having obtaining supplies. Recent budget cuts meant that they no longer held as large a stock of basic items in the unit and several times they had run out.

Max promised to look into it and the meeting broke up. Although the delivery rooms were empty, a couple of mums were due to be discharged that day so there was a lot to do. He tagged on the end as everyone filed out of the room. Lucy was in front of him and it struck him that it would be the ideal opportunity to have a word with her. If he had upset her, it would be better to get the problem out into the open rather than have it niggling away in the background all the time.

He caught up with her outside the office. 'Can I have a word with you, Lucy?'

'Of course.'

She turned to face him and Max was aware of a definite coolness about the look she gave him. Bearing in mind how well they had got on in the clinic, it seemed very strange, and he didn't waste time beating about the bush.

'Have I done something to upset you?'

'Of course not,' she replied quickly, but he saw the colour that touched her cheeks and knew that she was fibbing.

'Are you sure?' He smiled, hoping she would confide in him if he kept things low key. 'Because I get the distinct impression that I'm in your bad books for some reason.'

'You're imagining it. Now, if that's all, I really do need to get on.'

'Of course. But if I have upset you, Lucy, I apologise. The last thing I want is for us to be falling out.'

'There's nothing to apologise for,' she said tersely, turning away.

Max sighed as he watched her hurry along the corridor. Despite her protestations, he knew there was something wrong and it was frustrating not to be able to do anything about it. Exasperated with himself for letting it bother him, he went into the office and phoned the purchasing manager, not pulling his punches as he told him what he thought about the new system. It was rare he ever spoke so sharply but it paid dividends that day. The man immediately agreed to increase their stock limits and even promised to have extra supplies delivered by lunchtime.

Max hung up, knowing that he should be pleased that the matter had been resolved so speedily. However, it was hard to feel any pleasure when there seemed to be a cloud hanging over him. Maybe it was silly, but he hated to think that Lucy was annoyed with him. For some reason her opinion mattered to him more than anyone else's had done in a very long time.

Lucy went straight to the ward after she left Max. Sophie and baby Alfie were being discharged that morning and she wanted to say goodbye to them. Alfie had developed a mild case of jaundice after his birth and that was why he had been kept in. Extra fluids and phototherapy had soon cleared it up and he was now well enough to go home.

She pushed open the door, doing her best to calm herself down, but she could feel her nerves humming with tension. She hadn't known what to say when Max had asked if he'd upset her. She had never considered herself to be an overly demonstrative sort of person, so the fact that he had picked up on her mood had stunned her. Richard certainly hadn't noticed if she'd been upset. He'd been oblivious to anything that hadn't directly affected him, in fact. She definitely couldn't imagine

Richard worrying in case he'd offended her, let alone apologising for it!

Lucy frowned. It wasn't the first time she had found Richard lacking, yet in the beginning he had appeared so perfect. He'd been handsome, charming, witty, attentive—everything she could have wished for. It was only after they had started living together that she'd discovered he could be incredibly selfish at times too, but she'd been so sure that he was the man she'd wanted to spend her life with that she had made excuses for him.

Was she doing the same thing again? she wondered suddenly. All week long she had struggled to reconcile the impression she had formed of Max as a caring, dedicated doctor with the playboy bachelor Joanna had described. The only explanation she had come up with was that something must have happened in his past to make him behave so differently in his private life. It would be even easier to see that as the explanation after what had happened just now, too. Max had sounded genuinely concerned in case he had upset her, but Lucy realised it would be foolish to take it at face value. It was probably all part of his act, a way to project the right image!

Pain lanced her heart as she made her way to Sophie's bed. Even though she knew how silly it was, she couldn't help feeling disappointed. It was an effort to smile at the girl but the last thing Lucy wanted was anyone guessing how she felt. 'I've just popped in to say goodbye. I bet you're looking forward to going home, aren't you?'

'I suppose so,' Sophie muttered.

Lucy frowned when she heard the despondent note in Sophie's voice. 'What's the matter?'

'I'm just worried in case I can't cope,' Sophie admitted. 'I don't know anything about babies and there's so much to learn.'

'You'll be fine,' Lucy said encouragingly. 'All the staff have said how brilliant you are with Alfie. And they don't say that about all our mums, believe me!'

'I hope they're right,' Sophie said miserably, lifting her son out of the crib.

'They are,' Lucy said firmly, hating to hear the girl sounding so downhearted. 'I'm sure you'll be absolutely fine, but if you do have any concerns then ask your health visitor. She'll be visiting you every day for the next two weeks so you can discuss any problems with her. She'll also be able to tell you when the baby clinic is open. Don't forget that there are people there who can give you advice if you need it.'

'I suppose so.' Sophie still sounded very unsure. She cuddled Alfie for a moment and Lucy could see real fear in her eyes when she looked up. 'It's just a bit...well, *scary* knowing that I'm responsible for looking after him. I'm worried in case I do something wrong.'

'Most new mums feel like that,' Lucy assured her. 'Is there anyone at home who can help you?'

'No, there's nobody.'

'What about your family?' she persisted gently.

'My mum left home when I was a child and I haven't seen her since. My dad brought me up but he died last year.' Sophie's eyes filled with tears. 'I named Alfie after him.'

'I'm sure he would have been thrilled,' Lucy said kindly, passing her a tissue. 'What about Alfie's father? Will he help out?'

'I doubt it. He's left Dalverston and I've no idea where

he's living now.' Sophie blew her nose. 'He never wanted me to have Alfie in the first place. He was furious when I refused to have a termination. I'm glad he's gone because I don't want him anywhere near Alfie.'

'I understand,' Lucy said, feeling very sorry for the girl. She only wished there was something she could do to help her, but once Sophie left the maternity unit she was no longer their concern.

It wasn't an ideal situation by any means and Lucy couldn't help feeling concerned. 'I'll have to get back to work but don't forget that there's help available if you need it, Sophie. You only have to ask.'

'Thank you.'

Sophie dredged up a smile but Lucy could tell that she was still worried. She sighed as she made her way to the desk to see what Amanda wanted her to do. Even with daily visits from the health visitor, Sophie was going to find it hard work looking after Alfie by herself. New babies needed an awful lot of attention and with no family to call on, the girl would be very much on her own.

'Problems?'

She glanced up, feeling a wash of colour run up her cheeks when she realised that she had walked straight past Max without seeing him. Bearing in mind their earlier conversation, she felt obliged to stop. She didn't want him apologising again, not when it might start off all that soul-searching once more. Max might project the image of a caring, committed professional but she had to remember that it was all part of his act.

'I'm worried about Sophie Jones,' she said quickly, not wanting to dwell on that thought.

'Come into the office and tell me about it,' he said

immediately. He opened the office door, his brows rising when she hesitated. 'If you're worried about a patient, Lucy, we need to do something about it.'

'Of course.' She followed him into the room, pausing by the door as he walked over to the desk because it seemed wiser to maintain a little distance between them. When she was close to Max, it seemed to confuse things even more.

'OK, shoot.'

'It's nothing major,' she said quickly, refusing to allow the idea to take root. Max didn't present any danger to her when she knew exactly what he was like. 'I'm just a bit concerned because Sophie doesn't have anyone to help her when she gets home. I know there are lots of young mums living on their own who do a great job of bringing up their children, but most of them have someone they can call on for back-up. Sophie hasn't got anyone and she's admitted that she's worried in case she can't cope.'

'Hmm. It's a difficult situation and I understand why you're concerned,' Max said, frowning. He went over to the filing cabinet and pulled out Sophie's notes, shaking his head as he read through them. 'I wish I'd noticed this before. Look.'

Lucy went to join him, bending down so she could see what he was pointing to. 'There's no contact details, not even a name in the space for next of kin!'

'I know. Worrying, isn't it?'

He straightened up at the same moment as she did and she felt heat flash along her veins when their arms brushed. He'd rolled up his shirtsleeves and the feel of his skin against hers sent a surge of electricity shooting through her. Her eyes rose to his and her breath caught when she saw the awareness they held. Max had felt it too, felt that flash of heat, the tingling jolt of electricity that had sparked between them, and it was hard to hide her dismay as she hurriedly moved away.

What had happened with Richard had hit her hard. Her confidence in herself as an attractive, desirable woman had been rocked and it would be only too easy to use this as a much-needed boost, but at what cost? From what she had heard, Max cut a swathe through women, discarding them once they had outlived their usefulness. Could she accept that, or would she end up wanting more than he was prepared to offer?

Lucy bit her lip. She couldn't answer that question. It all depended on what she wanted from Max and she hadn't worked that out yet.

Max could feel his whole body throbbing. It wasn't a painful feeling but it was definitely worrying. He couldn't remember the last time he had reacted this strongly when he had touched a woman or if, indeed, it had ever happened. Surely it couldn't be a first?

He racked his brain but no matter how hard he tried he couldn't come up with another occasion when the feel of a woman's skin had instantly set him on fire. It hadn't even happened when he'd met his ex-wife, and the thought made him groan under his breath. What was it about Lucy that made him react this way?

Max had no idea what the answer was but he knew that he needed to put a rein on his feelings if he wasn't to make a fool of himself. He glanced at the file, hoping it would help if he focused on the current problem. There was no point torturing himself by recalling how Lucy had looked at him...

'I see that Sophie is registered with Dalverston

Surgery,' he said briskly, cutting off that thought. 'Rachel Thompson's her GP. That's good news.'

'You think it would be an idea to have a word with Dr Thompson about her?' Lucy said quietly.

Max felt a wave of tenderness wash over him when he heard the tremor in her voice. Although she was making a valiant effort, he could tell that she was as shocked by what had happened as he was. His own voice softened because he wanted her to know that there was nothing to worry about. Even if they were attracted to one another they would take things slowly; he definitely wouldn't rush her into his bed.

That was another thought that needed to bite the dust, fast. Max mentally ground it beneath his heel, praying that would be the last he heard of it. Getting hung up on the idea that Lucy would sleep with him was the last thing he needed!

'Yes, I do. Rachel set up an advisory service for teenage mums in Sophie's position a couple of years ago. Rachel was a teenage mum herself so she understands the problems better than most people do. I've heard a lot of good reports about the work they do.'

'What a brilliant idea!' Lucy exclaimed. 'I know we hold classes for all the new mums but it's impossible to cover everything in the time we can spend with them. The younger mums in particular could do with a lot more help.'

'That's why Rachel decided to set up this advisory service,' Max told her. 'I sat in on a session last year and it was excellent—good, sound advice presented in a way that the girls could understand but not feel as though they were being talked down to.'

'It's exactly what Sophie needs. She's very capable;

all the staff have said how good she is with Alfie. She just needs to gain a bit more confidence in herself.'

'Then the classes would be ideal for her. Another plus is that she'll meet other girls in her situation and hopefully make some friends. She won't feel quite so alone if she has someone her own age to talk to.'

'It's the perfect solution. Thanks, Max. I'll give Dr Thompson a call and see what she has to say.'

Lucy smiled at him, her whole face lighting up with delight, and Max felt another surge of heat flow through him and wash away every sensible thought he'd had. Maybe he didn't want to rush her, but he had to start somewhere.

'Look, Lucy,' he began, then stopped when the phone rang. He tried to curb his impatience as he reached for the receiver, but it was frustrating to be interrupted at such a crucial moment. 'Maternity. Max Curtis speaking.'

It was A and E requesting his assistance with a patient who'd been involved in an RTA. She was twenty weeks pregnant and bleeding heavily, and they needed him there, stat.

Max promised them he'd be straight there and hung up. He explained to Lucy that he had to go and left, sighing as he made his way to the lift. Another couple of seconds and he would have asked her out, but would that really have been the wise thing to do? Lucy wasn't the sort of woman he usually went out with. She would expect more from a relationship than a few casual dates, invest more of herself into it too. Was he prepared for that when it went against all his rules?

For the past three years, he had avoided commitment yet he knew in his heart that he wouldn't be able to do that with Lucy. Lucy made him dream about home and family, made him long for happily-ever-after, and they were all the things he could never have.

What he needed was a distraction to take his mind off her. It had been months since he'd been out on a date, now that he thought about it. He'd been too busy with work to worry about socialising and it was time he rectified that. There was a new nurse in A and E, who'd made it clear that she was interested in him; he would invite her out for dinner at the weekend.

As for Lucy, well, he would get over this crush or whatever it was in time. He had to. He certainly didn't intend to have his life disrupted all over again.

CHAPTER FIVE

THE day flew past. They had no sooner admitted Fiona Walker, the patient involved in the RTA, when two other mums phoned to say they were in labour. It meant they were really stretched to keep up but Lucy was glad because it gave her less time to brood about what had happened with Max. Maybe he did see her as an attractive and desirable woman, and maybe it was a boost to her confidence, but in her heart she knew it would be a mistake to get involved with him.

She had just escaped from one disastrous relationship and she needed to concentrate on putting her life back together. Perhaps a time would come when she felt able to trust a man again but not yet. And definitely not someone like Max. No matter how good he made her feel, Max was strictly off limits.

Lucy felt a little better after she had made her decision. By the time her shift ended, she felt much calmer about what had happened. Amanda was in the office when Lucy went to sign out; she looked up and grimaced.

'What a day! I couldn't believe it when those two mums turned up one after the other like that.'

'It has been hectic,' Lucy agreed. She filled in the

time next to her name then glanced at Amanda and frowned. 'Aren't you supposed to be off duty now as well?'

'I wish! I'm still trying to sort out the Christmas timetable,' Amanda explained. 'Every time I make a start on it, something happens, but I need to get it done soon.'

'Are you having problems finding people to work?' Lucy asked sympathetically.

'Yes. Normally, we use a rota system so that anyone who works nights over Christmas is off at New Year. Unfortunately, there aren't enough staff to do that this year.' Amanda sighed. 'Folk aren't going to be too pleased when they find out they're having to work both holidays.'

'I don't mind working,' Lucy offered. She shrugged when Amanda looked at her in surprise. 'I wasn't planning on doing anything so I may as well work.'

'Are you sure?' Amanda said uncertainly. 'I thought you'd want to go home and see your family.'

'No, it's fine. Really.' She smiled at the other woman, not wanting to explain why she preferred to remain in Dalverston. She had been dreading Christmas and the New Year, if she was honest. Her parents would expect her to go home and she couldn't face the thought of seeing everyone again. Working over the holidays would give her the perfect excuse to avoid it. 'You can put me down for Christmas and New Year if it helps.'

'Oh, it does!' Amanda assured her. She added Lucy's name to the timetable then printed out a copy and held it aloft. 'All done! Am I glad we hired you. I can't imagine anyone else volunteering to do a double stint of nights!'

'It isn't a problem,' Lucy said quickly, feeling a little uncomfortable when she would benefit from her offer far more than Amanda would. She picked up her bag and turned to leave. 'I'll be off, then. See you tomorrow.'

'Rightio... Oh, before I forget, what are you doing on Saturday night?'

Lucy paused. 'Nothing. Why?'

'A few of us have decided to go out for a pre-Christmas meal,' Amanda explained. 'It's just me, Joanna, Cathy and Margaret so far, although I'm hoping a couple of the community midwives will be able to join us. We're going to that Indian restaurant in the town centre so how do you fancy it?'

'I'd love to come,' Lucy agreed immediately. It was just what she needed, in fact, the first step towards building a social life. The first step towards taking her mind off Max, too. She hurriedly dismissed that thought. 'What time are you meeting up?'

'Seven o'clock outside the restaurant,' Amanda informed her, then looked up and smiled. 'Oh, good. I was hoping to catch you before you left. How do you fancy coming out for a curry on Saturday night?'

Lucy glanced round to see who Amanda was talking to and felt her heart jolt when she saw Max standing in the doorway. It was hard to maintain an outward show of calm as he came into the room. It wasn't just the fact that Max had seemed attracted to her that had shocked her, of course, but that she had reciprocated. Bearing in mind what had happened recently, she should have been immune to his appeal, but there was no point pretending. Even though she knew that Max was the last man she should get involved with, there was something about him that drew her.

Max could feel his body humming with tension as he walked into the office. He nodded to Lucy, hoping she couldn't tell how on edge he felt. Maybe he did intend to get over this…*crush* he seemed to have developed on her but it could take a little time. 'Sorry. I'm afraid I can't make it on Saturday. I've made other plans.'

'Oh, I see!' Amanda grinned at him. 'So who's the lucky lady, then? Don't tell me it's still that nurse from Paeds? She must be well past her sell-by date by now!'

Amanda laughed but Max was hard pressed to raise a smile. Even though he knew she hadn't meant any harm, he couldn't help feeling uncomfortable about Lucy hearing the comment. Although he was the first to admit that he'd been out with a lot of women, it wasn't nearly as many as people seemed to believe.

There was little he could do to redress the situation, unfortunately, so he changed the subject. 'I just came to see how Fiona Walker's been doing since she was transferred from A& and E. Has the bleeding stopped yet?'

'I'm not sure. Lucy has been monitoring her,' Amanda informed him.

'How is she?' Max repeated, turning to Lucy. He felt his heart give another unsteady lurch and had to batten it down, wondering exactly how long it would take to get things back onto a more even keel. The problem was that he had never experienced this kind of reaction before so he had no way of knowing if it would take days or even weeks. He sighed under his breath. Knowing that he could be in for a rough ride every time he spoke to her wasn't the most comforting prospect.

'The bleeding has eased off, although it hasn't

stopped. Diane did another ultrasound and the baby is still moving about so that's a good sign. And there's been no cramping either,' she added quietly.

'Good. All we can do is hope that everything settles down.' He turned to Amanda, determined to get a grip on himself. No matter how long it took, he knew what he needed to do. 'I'll be here for another hour at least so call me if there's a problem.'

'Will do, although it won't be me you hear from.' Amanda stood up. 'Thanks to Lucy, *I* am going home.'

'Lucy?' Max queried, wondering what she meant.

'Yes. Lucy has only gone and volunteered to work nights over Christmas *and* New Year.' Amanda picked up the timetable and showed it to him. 'I've been struggling to get this finished for days and now it's all sorted, thanks to her. She's a real star, wouldn't you agree, Max?'

'I...um...yes, of course.' Max summoned a smile, wondering why it bothered him so much to learn that Lucy had offered to work over the holidays. Surely she would want to be with her family at this time of the year, he thought. It was what he planned to do, spend time with his parents and brothers, and he couldn't understand why she didn't want to do that too...unless she preferred to remain in Dalverston rather than to go home and face whatever situation she had run away from.

His heart ached at the thought of what she must have been through but there was nothing he could do about it. He left the office and went to check on the two mums who'd been admitted that afternoon. One had just delivered a baby girl and there was nothing he needed to do except congratulate the parents. The other was well advanced with her labour and once again his services weren't needed. Diane was on call that night so technically he was free to leave. However, there was paperwork that needed doing first.

He went to the desk and entered Fiona Walker's notes into the computer. It was a job that Diane would normally have done but he'd never been one to worry unduly about protocol. He sighed as he printed out a copy for the patient's file, aware that it was merely an excuse. The truth was that he was filling in time because he didn't want to go home and spend the evening thinking about what had happened that day.

It was pointless going over it, time and time again. The fact was that Lucy wasn't right for him and he most definitely wasn't right for her. He had already taken the first step towards addressing the problem by asking someone else out and, hopefully, that should be the end of it. Once he got back into the swing of dating, he would forget about Lucy and the danger she presented to his peace of mind.

Lucy took her time getting ready on Saturday night. She had a long soak in the bath then washed and dried her hair, brushing the chestnut curls until they gleamed. It had taken her ages to decide what to wear but she'd finally decided on a jade-green top teamed with a pair of black trousers. High-heeled black patent shoes added a touch of elegance to the outfit as well as adding a welcome couple of inches to her height. When she stepped in front of the mirror, she couldn't help thinking that she looked more like herself than she had done in ages. The past six months had taken their toll but it felt as though she had turned a corner now. Moving to Dalverston had been the right thing to do, even if it had posed a few problems she had never anticipated.

Lucy clamped down on that thought as she fetched her coat and left the flat. There was no way that she was going to start thinking about Max again tonight. The restaurant was in the high street and she was able to walk there. Margaret and Joanna had already arrived and they decided to go inside to wait for the others rather than stand in the street. Amanda was the last to arrive, full of apologies for keeping them waiting.

'Sorry, sorry! My taxi didn't turn up and I had to phone for another one.' She draped her coat over a chair and sat down. 'Anyway, guess who I saw on my way here?'

'No idea,' Cathy piped up, handing her a menu. 'So come on, tell us—who did you see?'

'Only Max with that new nurse from A and E.' Amanda grinned when everyone gasped. 'That's not the best bit either. I saw them going into Franco's.'

'Franco's?' Margaret's brows shot up. 'It costs an arm and a leg in there. I should know because Jim took me there on my birthday and he's never stopped moaning about how much it cost him ever since!'

'It's the most expensive restaurant in town,' Amanda agreed. 'Max must have high hopes for the evening if he's coughing up that sort of money!'

Everyone laughed but Lucy found it impossible to join in. The thought of Max wining and dining the other woman as a prelude to spending the night with her was almost more than she could bear.

The thought seemed to cast a shadow over the evening. Far too often, she found herself wondering what Max was doing. Was he turning on the charm, steering the evening in the direction he wanted it to end? She sighed because it had nothing to do with her what he did. Max was a free agent and if he chose to sleep with every single nurse in the hospital that was up to him. She had no right to feel hurt when he was simply living up to his reputation, no rights at all where he was concerned. For some reason that thought made her feel even worse.

The evening proved to be less of a success than Max had hoped it would be. Normally, he enjoyed getting to know the women he dated. He genuinely liked women and was interested in finding out what made them tick. However, he found it hard to summon up any real enthusiasm that night.

He did his best, of course, but he was very aware that he was merely going through the motions. It was a relief when he could bring the evening to an end and drive his date home. He could tell that she was disappointed when he refused her offer of coffee but there was nothing he could do about it. The truth was that he wasn't interested in coffee or anything else that was on offer. Although sex may have been enough of an inducement at one time, it held little appeal for him now, and it was worrying to admit it.

He drove home and let himself into his apartment. Tossing his keys onto the sideboard, he took a long look around the place he'd called home for the past three years. Everywhere was perfect from the gleaming, pale wooden floors to the stark, white-painted walls. He'd bought the furniture as part of the package when he'd moved in: chunky black leather sofas; chrome and glass side tables; a state-of-the-art entertainment system. It was the archetypal bachelor pad and all of a sudden he loathed everything it represented.

This wasn't him, not the person he really was inside. He had been hiding behind this façade for the last three years and he couldn't hide behind it any longer. Discovering that he could never father a child had been a devastating blow. It had left him feeling as though he was less than a man and he had tried to compensate for that by having all those affairs. However, in his heart he knew that sex was no longer the answer.

He sank down onto the sofa as he forced himself to face the truth. He could sleep with a million women but it wouldn't change the way he felt about himself, certainly wouldn't change the facts. He would never be a father, never experience the joy of holding his own child in his arms. There would always be this huge gap in his life and nothing he did could make up for that.

It might have been different if he could have shared his sorrow with someone who loved him enough to bear the burden with him, but it wouldn't be fair to expect any woman to give up her dreams of motherhood for him. It was why his marriage had failed. Becky's feelings for him hadn't been strong enough to compensate for them not having a child. While Max didn't blame her for feeling that way, it hurt to know that he hadn't been enough for her, that she'd needed more. It made him see that it would take a very special woman to love him purely for himself.

Just for a second an image of Lucy appeared in his mind's eye before he dismissed it. There was no point going there. What he needed to do was to focus on the positive aspects of his life. He loved his job and couldn't wish for a more fulfilling career, but maybe it was time to set himself a new challenge. Once Anna was back from maternity leave, he would start applying for a permanent consultant's post, he decided. It would be a wrench to leave Dalverston, but a change of scene would do him good. He would make a fresh start somewhere else, maybe even think about moving abroad. His skills were in demand all over the world and he wouldn't have a problem finding a job. He would concentrate on his career and on making sure that the women who came to him delivered healthy babies.

It would be some compensation for what he could never have.

CHAPTER SIX

LUCY was on lates the following week, so she went into work at lunchtime on the Monday to find the maternity unit a hive of activity. With just two weeks left before Christmas, the staff had decided to put up some decorations and everywhere looked very festive. She smiled as she stopped to admire the nativity scene that had been arranged on the end of the reception desk.

'This is gorgeous. Where did you get it?'

'The husband of one of our mums made it for us,' Margaret told her. 'He's a carpenter by trade and he makes these in his spare time.'

'It's beautiful,' Lucy said, picking up one of the figures so she could admire the intricate carving.

'Apparently, he has a stall at the Christmas market,' Margaret explained, unravelling a shiny foil paper chain. 'I think I'll see if he has any left when I go into town tomorrow night. My grandchildren would love one.'

'I'm sure they would,' Lucy agreed, placing the figure back in its place. 'I'll just put my coat away and give you a hand if you like. I'm supposed to be showing some new mums around the unit today but they aren't due to arrive until two, which gives me plenty of time.'

'That would be great,' Margaret said gratefully.

'There's another box of decorations in the storeroom if you could fetch it on your way back.'

'Will do.'

Lucy put her coat in her locker then went to the storeroom and switched on the light. The box was on the top shelf and she had to stand on tiptoe to reach it. Hooking her finger under the edge of the carton, she eased it forward then gasped when it suddenly tumbled off the shelf.

'Careful!' All of a sudden Max was there. He deftly caught the box and placed it on the floor, shaking his head as he straightened up. 'Good job it didn't fall on top of you. It's really heavy.'

'I didn't realise that,' Lucy said shakily. She cleared her throat when she heard how strained she sounded but seeing Max so unexpectedly had thrown her. Even though she knew it hadn't anything to do with her, she couldn't help wondering if he had spent the weekend with that nurse he'd taken out on Saturday night.

'It's only supposed to be full of Christmas decorations,' she said hastily, not wanting to go down that route again. Far too often over the weekend she'd found herself thinking about what Max might be doing and she had to stop. 'I didn't think it would weigh so much.'

Max grimaced. 'It's heavy enough to give you a nasty bruise if it landed on you. I wonder what's in it.' Crouching down, he peeled off the sticky tape and opened the box. 'Ahah, there he is. I was wondering where good old Freddie had got to.'

He held up a garishly-coloured plastic reindeer. It had an eye missing and one antler was bent at a very odd angle. Lucy frowned when she saw it.

'Why on earth have the staff kept that thing? It's hideous!'

'Shh, mind what you say. You'll hurt poor Freddie's feelings,' Max admonished her. 'I'll have you know that Freddie is the unit's lucky mascot. So long as he's on duty then it's guaranteed that a baby will be born here over Christmas.'

Lucy burst out laughing. 'Bearing in mind how many of our mums are due to give birth in the next couple of weeks, I doubt if Freddie's services will be needed!'

'Take no notice of her, Freddie,' Max said firmly. He held up the reindeer and looked straight into its one good eye. 'She doesn't *mean* to be rude. She just doesn't understand your magical powers.'

'No, I don't,' Lucy agreed, smiling. The fact that Max was happy to play the fool showed her yet another side to his character and one that she found very appealing too. Richard had tended to stand very much on his dignity, but obviously Max didn't care a jot about that.

It was worrying to know that once again she had found things to admire about him and she hurried on. 'So how did Freddie acquire these magical powers?'

'I'm not sure how it happened. Maybe Santa had something to do with it,' he replied, completely deadpan. 'But ever since Freddie appeared on the scene, we've had a baby born in the unit on Christmas Day.'

'That's some record. I mean, from the look of him he must have been around for a very long time. I certainly can't remember seeing anything like him in the shops,' she added wryly.

'I don't expect you have,' Max agreed, grinning at her. 'Freddie is definitely a one-off.'

'You're not kidding! Why is he called Freddie,

though? I thought Rudolph was the only name for a reindeer.'

'Apparently, the staff named him after the head of the obstetrics department at the time.' He turned the reindeer around and pointed to its nose. 'Plus he doesn't have the requisite red nose to be called Rudolph.'

'Oh, I see.' Lucy chuckled. 'Right, so now that I know all about our illustrious Freddie, I'd better take him to Margaret. No doubt she has a special place all lined up for him,' she said, bending down to pick up the box.

'I'll carry that.'

Max gently moved her aside and Lucy sucked in her breath when she felt his hands gripping her arms. It was only the lightest of touches yet she was deeply aware of his fingers pressing into her flesh.

'I can manage,' she said, quickly straightening up.

'I'm sure you can but why struggle when you don't need to?'

Max lifted the box off the floor and she felt her heart give a tiny jolt when she saw the awareness in his eyes. Had he felt it too, she wondered giddily, felt that immediate heightening of the senses that always seemed to happen whenever they touched?

She knew it was true and it was scary to know that once again Max felt exactly the same as she did. As she followed him out of the storeroom she couldn't help wondering why it kept happening. What was it about him that made her feel this way? What was it about her that made him respond?

She had no idea what the answer was but she knew that she needed to be extra-vigilant. It would be only too easy to give in to this attraction they felt but it would be a mistake to do so. She'd had her heart broken once and she didn't intend to have it broken a second time.

Max may be attracted to her but she had to remember that was all it was. He wasn't interested in having a real relationship with her or any other woman.

Max carried the carton to the desk then made his apologies and left. He was meeting Diane later to go over her assessment and he wanted to run through a couple of points he needed to cover. He sighed as he let himself into the consultants' lounge because he knew it was just an excuse. He already knew what he wanted to say, but it had seemed wiser to put some distance between himself and Lucy.

He poured himself a cup of coffee and sat down, determined that he was going to master these feelings that kept running riot inside him whenever he was near her. He had enjoyed that brief conversation they'd had more than he had enjoyed the whole of Saturday night and it was worrying to realise the hold she was gaining over him. If it had been anyone except Lucy, he would have suggested they have an affair because it was obvious that she was attracted to him too. However, he was wary of doing that when he knew there could be repercussions.

Although he had no idea what had happened in her past, it was obvious that she had been hurt and he wouldn't risk it happening again. He also didn't intend to make the mistake of getting hurt himself. It made him see that the tentative plans he'd made about finding a consultant's post would need to be put into operation as soon as possible. If he had another job lined up when Anna returned from maternity leave, it would make life much simpler. He could move away from Dalverston and right away from temptation.

* * *

'We'll start with the delivery rooms first.'

Lucy opened the door to one of the suites and ushered her charges inside. Five mums had turned up for the tour and she smiled when she heard them gasp in surprise.

'It's much nicer than I thought it would be!' Rachel Green exclaimed. 'I was born at Dalverston General and my mum said the delivery room she was in was really horrible—all dark and dingy.'

'The maternity unit was rebuilt a few years ago,' Lucy explained. 'I wasn't here then, but I've seen photos of the old unit and this is much nicer.' She led the way to the en suite bathroom and switched on the light. 'Apparently, the facilities in the old unit had to be shared, but the new rooms are all en suite, so you have your own bath and a separate shower, plus loo.'

'I wish we had an en suite at home,' one of the other mums declared. 'I'm fed up with having to trail along the landing every time I need to go to the loo during the night. I must have got up at least a dozen times last night and I'm worn out!'

Everyone laughed at that. Lucy smiled when she heard them swapping stories about their own experiences. It was good for them to know that they weren't alone in suffering these minor discomforts.

'Is there a separate suite for water births?' Rachel Green asked once everyone had settled down. 'I've been wondering about a water birth but I wasn't sure if it was possible to have one here at Dalverston.'

'It is,' Lucy assured her. She crossed the room and pulled back a folding screen so they could see the birthing pool. 'Two of the suites are equipped with birthing pools, so it isn't a problem.'

'Oh, I'm not sure if I fancy a water birth,' one of the others said, grimacing.

'It's not for everyone,' Lucy agreed. 'Some women don't like the idea and others do. It's a matter of personal choice.'

'My mother-in-law is really against it,' Rachel told her, sighing. 'She keeps trying to persuade me to change my mind but I've read so many good reports about water births that I really fancy giving it a try.'

'A lot of women find that giving birth in water is less stressful. The buoyancy of the water helps to support them and makes it easier for them to relax. And that can make the whole process of giving birth far less painful.'

'What about the baby, though?' another mum asked. 'Isn't there a risk that it could drown?'

Lucy shook her head. 'No. The baby is still receiving oxygen via the umbilical cord when it's born, so being submerged under the water for a short time won't harm it. Once it's lifted out of the water then it will start to use its lungs to breathe.'

'What if there's a problem during the birth?' someone else piped up.

'Then we would ask the mum to get out of the pool,' Lucy explained. 'We carry out all the usual checks during the birth, so we would pick up on any problems if they occurred. And it goes without saying that if there was any indication beforehand that a water birth wasn't the right choice then we would advise against it.'

Everyone seemed happy with her answers, she was pleased to see. She was a firm believer in the benefits of a water birth and could only hope that it might encourage some of the other women to consider the idea. It obviously hadn't put Rachel off because she smiled happily.

'I'm going to tell David's mum all that the next time she starts going on about me having a *proper* birth. It might stop her nagging me to death!'

'But remember, Rachel, it's your choice, and you need to make that clear to her,' Lucy said firmly. 'Actually, I think we've got some leaflets about water births in the office. I'll give you one to take home. Maybe that will help to convince her.'

She made a note to fetch the leaflets after they'd finished their tour and carried on. They visited one of the wards next and once again everyone was impressed by the bright and airy facilities. After that, they went to the nursery and then the special care baby unit, where any sick babies were treated. Although they could have missed it out, Lucy knew that a lot of mums found it reassuring to learn that such facilities were available if necessary.

The women were a little subdued as they made their way back to the meeting room afterwards, but they soon brightened up after they'd had a cup of tea. Lucy left them to chat while she went to the office for the leaflets. Max was there, talking to Amanda, but he merely nodded when she went in and she didn't know whether to feel pleased or sorry.

She sighed as she headed back to the meeting room, wishing that she didn't feel so ambivalent. One minute she had decided to avoid him and the next she was disappointed because he hadn't spoken to her, and it was all very confusing. She knew that she needed to sort out her feelings, although what that would achieve was anyone's guess. It certainly wouldn't change the fact that Max's attitude to life was very different from her own.

Once the tour was over, it was time for Lucy to go for

her break. There were just her and Cathy on duty that evening and she was hoping it wouldn't be too busy. She had just got back when Anita Walsh, one of the community midwives, phoned to say that she was sending a patient in to them. Anita was on her way back from visiting another of her mums and was stuck in traffic. She promised to get there as soon as she could, but in the meantime she would be grateful if someone would look after her patient for her.

Lucy assured her that she would sort everything out. She made her way to Reception and a few minutes later Emma Baker and her husband arrived. She booked Emma in then showed the couple to the delivery suite they'd be using. It was Emma's third child and she was very matter-of-fact about the birth. She was only due to stay in the unit for six hours following the birth and would be sent home after that so long as everything went smoothly.

Lucy did Emma's obs then set up the foetal monitor to check the baby's progress. She was a little concerned when she discovered that its heartbeat was much slower than it should have been. It was a sign that the baby could be in distress due to a lack of oxygen and needed monitoring.

She decided to wait a couple of minutes and do another foetal heart tracing as it could turn out to be a temporary blip. Emma's contractions were strong and the tightening of her uterus could have reduced the supply of oxygen reaching the baby via the placenta. She got everything ready then did another tracing of the baby's heartbeat, along with a recording of the uterine contractions. Checking it back, she was in no doubt that the baby was becoming increasingly distressed.

'Is something wrong?' Emma asked after she'd finished.

'I'm not happy about the baby's heart rate,' Lucy explained gently. 'It's slower than it should be, which means your baby is starting to show signs of distress.'

'But this didn't happen with the other two,' Emma protested. She turned to her husband. 'Did it, Peter?'

'No, it didn't,' he stated emphatically. 'Are you sure that machine is working properly?'

'There's nothing wrong with the equipment,' Lucy assured him. She could tell they weren't happy with her findings but there was little she could do about it. The baby was her first concern and she knew that she needed a doctor to take a look at it.

Lucy explained all this to Emma, then went to the phone and asked the switchboard to page Diane. The registrar phoned her back almost immediately to say that she was with a patient who was threatening to miscarry and didn't know how long she would be. She suggested that Lucy page Max if it was urgent.

Lucy sighed as she contacted the switchboard again. Although she would have liked a little more breathing space before she saw Max again, obviously it wasn't to be. She would just have to play it cool and not allow herself to get carried away. Max may be an extremely attractive man but she wasn't about to embark on another disastrous relationship. She had learned her lesson the hard way and she wasn't going to repeat her mistakes.

Max was on his way out of the hospital when his pager beeped. He groaned as he turned round and headed back inside. So much for hoping he might get an early finish for once, he thought ruefully as he made his way to the lift. Lucy met him in the corridor and he had to make a determined effort not to react when he saw her standing there. However, he couldn't deny that his heart seemed to be kicking up a storm and it was annoying after he had resolved to behave sensibly from now on.

'Did you want me?' he asked, adopting a deliberately neutral tone.

'Yes. I need you to take a look at a patient for me, please.' She led the way to the delivery room and paused outside the door to hand him the printout from the foetal monitor. 'As you can see from this, the baby is showing signs of distress. It's the mother's third child and she's roughly six centimetres dilated, but I wasn't happy about waiting.'

'It could be a while yet before the baby is born,' Max agreed, glancing at the tracing. He reached past her to open the door, feeling his senses spin when he realised all of a sudden just how petite she was. Her head barely came up to his shoulder yet for some reason he had never noticed it before. It was difficult to concentrate as he followed her into the room when at every turn he seemed to discover something new and fascinating about her.

'Dr Curtis would like to take a look at you, Emma,' Lucy explained as she led him over to the bed.

Max dredged up a smile, determined that he was going to get a grip on himself. 'Lucy tells me that your baby appears to be a little distressed, Emma. I'd just like to examine you and see what's happening, if you don't mind.'

Emma didn't look too happy as he gently examined her, feeling her tummy first so that he could check the position of the baby in case that was the cause of the problem. Everything was exactly as it should be; the baby was lying with its head well down, in a perfect position to be born.

'That's fine,' Max said moving to the bottom of the bed. 'Baby's in a good position so that isn't the problem.'

'We never had anything like this happen with the other two,' Emma's husband said curtly. 'Are you sure there really is a problem?'

'I'm afraid so. I know it must be hard to accept after you've had two trouble-free births, but trust me when I say that we all want the same thing. We want to make sure that your baby is safe and well.'

He carried on with his examination when the couple didn't raise any further objections, frowning when he spotted a loop of the umbilical cord protruding down through the mother's cervix. 'Take a look at this,' he said softly to Lucy.

She bent down to look and nodded. 'I see what you mean, although it wasn't there before.'

'It's probably slipped further down as the baby's moved down the birth canal.'

Max straightened up, knowing that there was no time to delay. 'A loop of the umbilical cord is protruding down through your cervix, Emma. It means there's a very real danger that your baby could be deprived of oxygen. The safest way to avoid that happening is to perform a section.'

'A section!' Emma exclaimed in dismay. 'You mean you want to operate?'

'Yes. If you were fully dilated, I might have recommended a forceps delivery but we can't afford to wait. A section will be quicker and safer.'

'I don't know… I mean, I never imagined anything would go wrong.' Emma bit her lip. It was obvious that she was upset at the thought of having her baby delivered by Caesarean section when she'd expected to have a normal birth.

'Dr Curtis wouldn't suggest a section unless he was absolutely sure it was the best thing to do,' Lucy said quietly.

Max felt his heart lift when he heard the conviction in her voice. There wasn't a doubt in his mind that she meant what she said and the fact that she so obviously trusted his judgement filled him with joy. He cleared his throat, not wanting her to suspect how moved he felt by her vote of confidence.

'Lucy's right. I am not an advocate for stepping in unnecessarily, believe me. However, there are occasions when it would be foolish not to do so. Your baby could suffer permanent brain damage if he's deprived of oxygen and that is a risk I'm sure none of us wishes to take.'

'No, of course not,' Emma agreed shakily. 'I'd never forgive myself if that happened. If you think a section is necessary then that's what we'll do. Isn't that right, Peter?'

'I…um…yes, of course,' her husband muttered, looking a little shocked.

Max wasted no more time as he went to the phone and informed Theatre that he would be operating. In a very short time, Emma was on her way. He followed the convoy out of the room, pausing briefly to have a last word with Lucy. 'The baby should be fine and so will Emma. She'll be back with you in no time at all.'

'Thank you. I know they're in safe hands.'

Max felt that little tug on his emotions again. Why did her opinion matter so much? he wondered. He knew he was good at his job and didn't need anyone to tell him that, yet it meant something really special to know that she believed in him.

He shrugged, trying not to get too hung up on the idea. 'As I've said before, we make a good team, Lucy. I doubt if Emma would have agreed to this op so readily without your input. She was obviously swayed by the reference you gave me.'

She gave a little grimace but he saw the colour that tinted her cheeks. 'I only told her the truth.'

'Then thank you.' His voice dropped and he could hear the emotion it held even if she couldn't. 'It's good to know that you have such faith in me, Lucy.'

He turned away, knowing that he was in danger of saying too much. It would be a mistake to do that, a huge mistake to let himself get carried away. He sighed as he headed for the lift. A few kind words and he was like putty in her hands!

CHAPTER SEVEN

LUCY popped into the special care baby unit to see Emma's baby before she went home. Although little Ruby Rose Baker didn't appear to have suffered any ill-effects from what had happened, it was normal practice to keep any babies born by Caesarean section in the unit for the first couple of days. Anita Walsh, the community midwife, was there when she arrived.

'I can't believe this has happened!' Anita exclaimed. 'It was a textbook pregnancy from the start, just like Emma's previous two were. She didn't even suffer from morning sickness!'

'No wonder she was so stunned when she was told that she needed a section,' Lucy said sympathetically. 'It must have been a real shock for her.'

'It was. She was only expecting to stay in for a few hours and now she'll be here for a week.' Anita sighed. 'I know how stubborn Emma can be when she sets her mind on something, so I expect she kicked up a bit of a fuss. I'm really sorry that you got landed with this, Lucy.'

'It wasn't your fault,' she assured her. 'Anyway, Emma seemed to accept what needed to be done once Max had explained how dangerous it could be for the baby.'

'Now, that I can believe,' Anita said with a laugh.

'Not many women can resist when Max turns on the charm!'

Lucy smiled dutifully but it was painful to have Max's reputation as a silver-tongued charmer confirmed once more. She tried to shake off the feeling of disappointment that filled her as they left the unit, but it was hard to shift it. Although she knew how foolish it was, she didn't want to have to see Max in anything other than a positive light.

'So how are you settling in?' Anita asked as they headed along the corridor. 'It must be a big change for you living here after the city. I'm not sure if I could make the move the other way.'

'I really like it here,' Lucy replied truthfully, glad to have something other than Max to occupy her thoughts. 'I certainly don't feel as though I'm missing out by not being surrounded by all the hustle and bustle of city life.'

'What about your friends and family, though? You must miss them,' Anita suggested.

'I do, but it's easier for everyone if I'm living here,' she said without thinking.

'What do you mean by that?' Anita asked in surprise.

Lucy sighed when she saw the curiosity on the older woman's face. Although she didn't want to go into detail about what had led her to leave Manchester, she could hardly refuse to answer. 'Oh, just that I split up with my fiancé a few months ago and it caused a bit of a stir. That was the reason why I decided to move to Dalverston, in fact. I wanted to make a completely fresh start.'

'Oh, dear, I am sorry.' Anita patted her hand. 'It can't have been easy for you, Lucy, but I'm sure you did the right thing.'

'I'm sure I did too.' Lucy summoned a smile, although she couldn't help wondering if she was right to say that.

She sighed as she said goodbye to Anita and went to fetch her coat because she knew what was behind her doubts. It was this situation with Max that troubled her and until she had worked out what to do about it, it would continue to do so. It was worrying to think that she had escaped from one difficult situation only to jump straight into another.

It was almost eight p.m. before Max was ready to leave. After he'd finished in Theatre, Diana had paged him about her patient. By the time they had discussed possible courses of treatment, he'd needed to check on Emma Baker again. Still, the upside was that he'd been far too busy to think about Lucy.

He groaned as he made his way across the car park. Every thought he had these days was followed by another one about Lucy and it was scary to know how hung up he was on her. Maybe he had made plans to address the situation, but it was the here and now that worried him, what would happen in the next few weeks. Although he'd had no problem avoiding commitment in the last three years, it was different with Lucy, very different indeed, and that's what worried him. He simply couldn't trust himself to do the sensible thing.

It was a disquieting thought and he found it impossible to shrug it off as he got into his car. There was a Christmas market being held in the town that week and there was a lot of traffic about when he left the hospital so it took him twice as long as normal to reach the town centre. The market was being held in the main square and the traffic was even worse there because of the numerous diversions that had been set up to avoid it. Max followed the signs, wishing that he had stayed in work until the market closed. At this rate he'd still be driving around at midnight!

He had just reached the junction with the main road when he spotted a commotion on the pavement. A young woman had collapsed and a crowd was starting to gather around her. Pulling into the kerb, he jumped out of his car and hurried over to see if he could help.

'I'm a doctor,' he explained as he pushed his way through the bystanders. He crouched down next to a young man who was obviously with the woman and introduced himself. 'My name's Max Curtis and I'm a doctor at Dalverston General. Is there anything I can do to help?'

'It's my wife. She…she's having a baby!'

The man looked as though he was ready to keel over at any second so Max moved him aside. He smiled at the young woman. 'My name is Max Curtis and I'm a doctor. As luck would have it, I work in the maternity unit at Dalverston General.'

'Thank heavens for that!' she exclaimed.

'Can you tell me your name and when your baby's due?' he asked, checking her pulse.

'Alison Cooper and my baby *was* due on New Year's Day, although I don't think he's going to wait that long,' she added ruefully.

'So how long have you been having contractions?' he continued, wanting to build up a clearer picture of what was happening.

'I'm not sure. I've been having pains on and off for a couple of days but I assumed they were Braxton Hicks' contractions. I wanted to visit the Christmas market tonight, so we drove over here from Ulverston, but as we were walking back to the car, my waters broke.'

'And how long ago did that happen?'

'About ten minutes,' she began, then groaned as another contraction started.

Max checked his watch, needing to know how frequent her contractions were. He also needed to examine her, although he was loath to do so with all these people watching. He was just trying to work out how to afford her some privacy when he heard someone calling his name and glancing round he saw Lucy pushing her way through the crowd.

'What are you doing here?' he demanded, feeling his heart squeeze in an extra beat as she crouched down beside him.

'I just got off the bus and saw the crowd. Somebody said that a woman had gone into labour, so I came to see if I could help. I take it that someone has phoned for an ambulance?'

'I did,' Alison's husband told them anxiously. 'It's taking ages to get here, though.'

Max bit back a sigh. With the amount of traffic on the roads that night it could be a while before an ambulance arrived. In the meantime, he and Lucy would have to deal with the situation. He turned to her, trying not to notice how pretty she looked in the light from the streetlamp, but that was like trying not to notice if the sun was shining. Every cell in his body seemed attuned to her as they crouched side by side on the pavement and his racing heart seemed to race that little bit faster. It was hard to appear the calm professional when his emotions seemed intent on doing their own thing.

'We need to examine her but not here with everyone watching. Can you find somewhere close by which would give us some privacy?'

'Of course.' She looked around then pointed towards a row of shops across the road. 'I'll see if anyone has a room they will let us use.'

'Great. Thanks, Lucy.'

'No problem.'

She gave him a quick smile as she stood up. Max let himself bask in its glow for a second before he turned his attention back to Alison. There was a time and a place for everything, he reminded himself sternly, although maybe that wasn't the best advice. He was trying to *avoid* getting involved with her, not staving off the moment until a later date!

Lucy could feel her heart racing as she hurried across the road and sighed. It wasn't just the adrenalin rush from dealing with this situation that was causing it to happen. It was being with Max that made her feel so keyed up. Maybe she didn't intend to get involved with him but it was proving harder than it should have been to stick to that.

She pushed the thought to the back of her mind as she hurried into the first shop she came to, which happened to be a sweet shop. The shop keeper, an elderly woman, had been watching what was happening through the window and came hurrying to meet her.

'Is that young woman all right? I'm on my own in here, otherwise I'd have gone out to see if I could help.'

'She's fine, or she will be if we can get her somewhere a little more private,' Lucy explained. 'She's having a baby and the pavement isn't the best place for that.'

'Good heavens!' the old lady exclaimed. 'A baby? Really?'

'Yes. I know it's a lot to ask but do you have a room we could use? An ambulance is on its way but it could take some time to get here with all the traffic. It would be better if she could wait somewhere a little less public.'

'Of course, dear. You can use the storeroom.'

The old lady opened a door and showed her the storeroom. Although it was full of boxes, it was warm and clean and would be perfect for their needs. Lucy thanked her and hurried back to tell Max the good news.

'We can use the storeroom in the sweet shop. It's ideal for what we need.'

'Good.' He lowered his voice. 'I don't think this baby is going to wait for the ambulance to arrive so let's get her inside as quickly as we can.'

They helped Alison to her feet and then with Max supporting her on one side and her husband on the other, they led her over to the shop. They had to stop halfway when another contraction began and Lucy could understand Max's eagerness to get her inside. The old lady had found some clean towels and laid them on the floor to form a makeshift bed and they quickly got Alison settled. Lucy helped Alison out of her underclothes and waited while Max examined her. The baby's head was already crowning and she knew it wouldn't be long before it was born.

'It's not going to be long now,' Max confirmed, smiling at Alison. 'It must be every child's dream to be born in a sweet shop, I imagine.'

Alison laughed. 'It's not what I had planned, believe me.'

She broke off when another contraction began. Lucy

beckoned to her husband and told him to sit down beside her and hold her hand. He still looked very shaky and the last thing they needed was him fainting. As soon as the contraction ended, she turned to Alison.

'I want you to wait until you feel another contraction begin before you try to push this time.'

'But I want to push now!' Alison exclaimed.

'I know you do, but you'll only tire yourself out if you try to push too soon. You need to work with your contractions and use them to help you deliver your baby.'

Alison did her best to follow their instructions and in a very short time the baby's head emerged. Lucy gently supported the head as it turned until it was once more in line with the baby's body. After another couple of contractions first one shoulder and then the other were delivered before the rest of the baby slid out into her hands. Lucy laughed when the child let out an angry wail.

'Congratulations! You have a beautiful little boy. And he obviously has a fine pair of lungs from the sound of it.'

She gently cleaned the baby's face with one of the towels then placed him on Alison's tummy, smiling when she saw the awe on the parents' faces as they saw their son for the first time. She glanced at Max, wanting to share the moment with him, and was shocked by the emotion she saw in his eyes. He was staring at the child with such longing that she felt her heart ache, even though she had no idea what was going on.

There was no time to ask him either as the sound of a siren announced the arrival of the ambulance. The crew carried a birthing kit on board so once the cord had been clamped and cut, and the placenta expelled,

Alison was placed on a stretcher and loaded on board. Lucy wrapped the baby in a blanket and placed him in his mother's arms.

'You did brilliantly, Alison. Not many women would have coped so well in the circumstances. You should be proud of yourself.'

'Thank you. Although I wouldn't have managed half so well if you and Max hadn't been there,' Alison told her sincerely.

'It was our pleasure.' Lucy ran her finger down the baby's soft little cheek then climbed out of the ambulance. The crew closed the doors and that was that. She sighed as she watched the vehicle making its way along the road. 'Talk about being in the right place at the right time.'

'It was fortunate,' Max agreed, but she could hear the grating note in his voice and once again found herself wondering about what she had witnessed.

Bearing in mind Max's reputation as a womaniser, she would never have imagined that he would be keen to have a child of his own. However, there was no doubt about what she had seen and she had to admit that she was intrigued. She longed to ask him what was going on, yet at the same time she knew it could be a mistake to do so. Her emotions had been all over the place recently, so could she risk getting drawn into a situation she might not be able to handle?

It was the uncertainty that scared her most of all, the fact that she couldn't answer that question with any degree of assurance. She sighed softly. In her heart she knew that it would be better if she left things alone rather than delve any deeper, yet it was hard to do that.

The truth was that she hated to think that Max might be suffering and not be able to do anything to help him.

Max could feel the flood of emotions that had hit him as he had watched Alison's baby being born swirling around inside him. He had honestly believed that he had come to terms with the fact that he would never have a family of his own, but he couldn't deny the yearning he'd felt just now and it filled him with sadness. There was no point wishing for the impossible, no point at all hoping that a miracle would happen. He would never father a child and that was the end of the matter.

He turned to Lucy, trying to ignore the nagging ache in his heart. 'I'll give you a lift home.'

'There's no need. Really.' She glanced along the road and shrugged. 'There doesn't seem much point in you trying to find a way through all this traffic when it'll only take me a couple of minutes to walk home from here.'

Max appreciated the sense of what she was saying, but all of a sudden he was loath to let the evening end there. Maybe it was foolish, but he knew that spending some time with her would help him deal with this sorrow he felt. 'In that case, how do you fancy having a look around the market? It's open until ten so there's plenty of time left. I don't know about you, but I could do with chilling out after everything that's happened tonight.'

'I'm not sure,' she began, but he didn't let her finish. The thought of sitting on his own in the flat with all these thoughts whizzing around his head was more than he could bear.

'Please say you'll come. We can wander around for a

while and soak up the atmosphere. It will be the perfect stress-buster after such a hectic day.'

She sighed softly. 'Anita was right. You can be very persuasive when you choose.'

Max laughed although he wasn't sure if the comment had been meant as a compliment. 'I won't ask you why she said that. All I can say is that I'd really enjoy your company, Lucy.'

She hesitated a moment longer then shrugged. 'All right, then, I'll come. But what about your car? You can't leave it here in case it gets towed away.'

'Good point.' Max frowned, hating to think that his plans might be scuppered by the lack of a parking space. His expression cleared as his gaze alighted on the sweet shop. 'I know, I'll ask the lady in the sweet shop if I can park it at the side of her shop. Hang on a moment while I see what she says.'

It took just a couple of minutes to arrange to leave his car in the alley next to the shop. Despite the lateness of the hour, there were still crowds of people milling about as he and Lucy made their way to the town square. The market stalls looked very festive with strings of brightly coloured lights hanging from their awnings. Max stopped when they came to a stall that was selling roasted chestnuts and sniffed appreciatively.

'Now, this is what Christmas smells like to me. Mum always used to buy us hot chestnuts when we were kids and it really takes me back to my childhood whenever I smell them.'

'I've never had chestnuts,' Lucy admitted, grinning when he gasped in feigned horror. 'Obviously, I was a deprived child, although don't tell my mum I said that or she'll have a fit!'

'Your secret is safe with me. Cross my heart and hope to die,' he promised with due solemnity, drawing a cross on his chest with his finger.

Lucy chuckled. 'I don't expect you to go to such extremes to guard my secret, Max.'

'That's a relief,' he declared, grinning at her. He dug in his pocket for some change and bought two bags of chestnuts, handing her one of them. 'Careful, they're hot.'

Lucy grimaced as she juggled the bag from hand to hand. 'You're not joking. My fingers are already singed!'

'Here.' Max took the bag from her and popped it in his pocket. 'We'll share this bag first,' he told her, lifting out a plump chestnut. He quickly peeled it and handed it to her, then peeled another for himself.

'Mmm, this is delicious.' She licked her fingers then held out her hand. 'Can I have another one, please?'

Max laughed. 'You made short work of that for someone who's never tasted chestnuts before.'

'There's a first time for everything,' she assured him cheekily, waggling her fingers under his nose.

Max chuckled as he peeled her another chestnut. They wandered around the market while they ate them, looking at the various stalls. Lucy stopped to admire some delicate glass ornaments, shaking her head when he suggested she buy one.

'There's no point,' she explained, putting the ornament back in its box. 'I'm not having a tree this year, and as I'm not going home, there's no point buying one for my parents either.'

Max frowned when he heard the sadness in her voice. Even though it had been her decision to work over the holiday, he could tell that she was upset about not spending time with her family. It made him wonder once again what had happened to make her decide not to go home. It must have been an extremely painful experience if she preferred to cut herself off from the people she loved.

The thought lingered at the back of his mind as they carried on. When they came to a stall that was selling mulled wine, Lucy stopped.

'Now, this is what reminds *me* of Christmas. Mum makes mulled wine every year on Christmas Eve. My sister and I always used to leave a glass for Santa to go with his mince pie.'

'And did he drink it?' Max asked, loving the way her eyes had lit up at the memory.

'Of course—or at least somebody did.' She grinned at him. 'Dad reckons that Christmas isn't the same since Laura and I stopped believing in Father Christmas, so let's just say that I have my suspicions.'

Max laughed. 'Well, I think you and your sister should reinstate the tradition. After all, you can't *prove* that Father Christmas doesn't exist, can you? Maybe he still pops in but doesn't leave you any presents these days because you're all grown up.'

'That's exactly what my dad said,' she told him, rolling her eyes. 'You men certainly stick together!'

'Can I help it if we take a more logical view of matters?' he said, spreading his hands wide open in a gesture of innocence.

'Logical? You class hedging your bets in case Father Christmas actually does exist as an example of superior male logic? Oh, *please*!'

'Until someone comes up with proof that Santa is a

myth then I intend to keep a completely open mind on the subject,' he declared loftily.

'I suppose you feel the same about the Tooth Fairy and the Easter Bunny?' she retorted and he grinned.

'But of course.'

She shook her head. 'You are completely mad, do you know that?'

'Not mad, just reluctant to let all the magic disappear from my life.' He smiled at her. 'There are worse sins than clinging onto the things that make childhood such a wonderful time.'

'You're right, there are,' she conceded.

Max felt his breath catch when she smiled up at him. When she looked at him that way it was hard to remember that he was supposed to be acting sensibly and the temptation proved just too great. Bending, he placed his mouth over hers. Her lips were cool from the night air yet he could sense the heat beneath the chill and groaned. Kissing Lucy was like nothing he had ever experienced before!

His lips clung to hers, demanding a response, and a surge of delight rushed through him when he felt her kiss him back. He had no idea how long they would have stood there if the sound of laughter hadn't reminded him that they were standing in the middle of the square with people milling about all around them. He drew back reluctantly, seeing the shock in her eyes, and knew that she was as stunned by what had happened as he was.

'I suppose I should apologise, although I'm not sorry that I kissed you,' he said truthfully. 'I've been wanting to do it for ages.'

'Have you?' she whispered, her voice catching.

'Yes.' Reaching out he brushed his knuckles over her

mouth and felt her shudder. There was a definite tremor in his voice when he continued. 'There's just something about you, Lucy, that draws me, even though I know how crazy it is.'

'Because you don't do commitment?'

'No, I don't.' He sighed, wishing he could explain why he lived his life the way he did. He just couldn't bear to think that she might view him differently if he told her the truth about himself. Would she consider him to be less of a man if she found out that he couldn't father a child, he wondered, or, worse still, *pity* him? He had no idea and he wasn't about to risk finding out.

'I'm far too busy with my career to devote the time it needs to a long-term relationship,' he explained, aware that he was taking the coward's way out. Although his career was important to him, it wasn't the real reason why he had avoided getting involved these past three years.

'I understand, Max, and it isn't a problem.' She shrugged when he looked at her. 'I'm not interested in having a long-term relationship either.'

'You're not?' he queried, unable to hide his surprise.

'No. I won't bore you with the details. Suffice to say that I don't plan on getting involved with anyone again for a very long time, if ever. So don't worry, Max. I'm certainly not holding out for the happily-ever-after, if that's what worries you!'

CHAPTER EIGHT

LUCY couldn't believe she'd said that. Panic gripped her as she ran the words through her head again. They sounded less like a statement than an invitation to have an affair, and that wasn't what she wanted...

Was it?

Desire rushed through her as she recalled the heat of Max's mouth when it had closed over hers. His lips had drawn a response from her that she'd been powerless to refuse and that had never happened before. Not once in all her life had she been swept away by passion, never had she felt such hunger or such need. Max's kiss had aroused her in ways that no man's kisses had ever done, not even Richard's.

The shock of that discovery made her gasp and she saw Max look at her in concern. 'Lucy? Are you all right?'

Lucy struggled to get a grip on herself. She had truly believed that she had been in love with Richard but how could she have been if his love-making had left her unmoved? 'I'm fine. Just a bit tired after everything that's happened tonight.'

'We both know that isn't true! At least be honest with me if nothing else. You're upset because I kissed you, aren't you?'

'Yes, but not in the way you mean.' She looked him straight in the eyes. Maybe she would regret this later but she wouldn't lie to him. As he had said, the very least they could do was to be honest with each other. 'I'm not upset because you kissed me, Max, but because of how it made me feel.'

'And how did it make you feel?' he asked, his voice grating in a way that made a shiver dance down her spine.

'More alive than I've ever felt before.'

'That's how I felt, too.'

'Is it?'

'Yes. So where do we go from here, Lucy?'

Lucy bit her lip because she had no idea what to say. If she told him the truth, that she wanted him to kiss her again and not only kiss her either but make love to her, she didn't know where it would lead. Max had made it clear that he wasn't interested in commitment, but could she have a purely physical relationship with him while remaining emotionally detached? Although she had sworn that she wouldn't get involved with a man again, she was no longer sure if she could stick to that. Not with Max.

'I don't know,' she said candidly. 'I really don't know where we go from here, do you?'

'No.' He sighed. 'It would be only too easy to make the wrong decision, wouldn't it? Maybe it would be best if we called a halt right now rather than find ourselves in a situation we both live to regret.'

'It seems the most sensible thing to do,' she agreed softly, hoping he couldn't hear the hurt in her voice. Maybe it did make sense, but she couldn't pretend that it didn't upset her to know that he could dismiss what had happened with such ease.

'I think it's time I went home,' she said quickly before she ended up saying something that would embarrass him. Max may have enjoyed kissing her but it certainly hadn't been enough to make him change his whole outlook on life. 'Thank you for the chestnuts. I really enjoyed them.'

'I'm glad.' He smiled at her, his brown eyes filled with a warmth that made her heart ache. It would be only too easy to see it as a sign that he really cared about her but it would be a mistake. 'Thank you for spending the evening with me, Lucy. I wouldn't have missed it for the world.'

'Me too,' she admitted huskily. She felt her breath catch when he bent towards her, but he merely kissed her on the cheek before he stepped back.

'Are you sure you'll be all right walking home on your own?'

'I'll be fine,' she assured him, quelling the feeling of disappointment that filled her. 'The one advantage of living so close to the town centre is that it only takes me a couple of minutes to walk home.'

'That's good, I suppose, although I have to confess that I wouldn't fancy living where you do.'

She shrugged. 'Needs must, I'm afraid. I have to watch every penny I spend at the moment.'

Max frowned. 'So that's why you opted to live there?'

'Yes.' She summoned a smile when she saw the concern on his face. The last thing she wanted was him thinking that she was looking for sympathy. 'Anyway, it's not nearly as bad as it looks.'

'If you say so.'

Lucy could tell he wasn't convinced but there was nothing she could do about it, so she said goodbye and left. Most of the stalls were closing up for the night and people were drifting away. As she made her way home, she couldn't help wondering what might have happened if Max hadn't decided they should call a halt. Would he have wanted to come back to her flat and spend the night with her? Would she have let him?

She sighed because there was no point going down that route. From now on she had to think of Max simply as a colleague, no matter how difficult it was going to be.

The next few days passed in a whirl of activity. Max knew that he was deliberately keeping himself busy so that he didn't have time to think about what had happened. Although he was sure that he had made the right decision, it didn't make it any easier. Having experienced the wonder of that kiss he and Lucy had shared, his body continually craved more.

In an effort to break the cycle, he finished early on Friday and went to visit his parents. He was hoping that the change of scene would do him good, but far too often during the weekend he found himself thinking about Lucy and it was worrying to realise the hold she had over him.

He knew that he had to do something about it, so as soon as he got home on the Sunday he went through all the recent copies of the medical journals he subscribed to. There were a couple of consultants' posts that sounded promising so he ringed them in red then sat down to update his CV. Once that was done, he wrote covering letters, popped everything into envelopes and took them to the post box. He felt much better afterwards, more settled. He was doing something positive about the situation, giving himself a reason to keep away from Lucy, and that had to be a good thing.

He went into work the following day, feeling a lot more upbeat. Amanda was on duty and she grimaced when she spotted him walking towards the desk.

'You certainly know when to take time off! If I didn't know better, I'd think you possessed second sight or something.'

'Why? What's happened?'

'Where do you want me to begin? First of all Margaret slipped on a patch of ice on Friday night and sprained her ankle, and then Joanna phoned yesterday to say that she had a rash all over her face and didn't know if she should come into work.' Amanda rolled her eyes. 'I told her to see her GP this morning and she's just rung up to say that he thinks it's German measles.'

'I see.' Max frowned. Although German measles, or rubella to give it its proper name, was a relatively mild viral infection, it could cause serious repercussions for a baby if the mother caught it in the early stages of pregnancy. He couldn't help feeling concerned. 'When was the last time that Joanna worked in the antenatal clinic?'

'The end of November. I checked on that as soon as she told me what her GP had said,' Amanda informed him.

'She wouldn't have been infectious then,' he said in relief. 'The virus can only be transmitted from a few days before any symptoms appear until one day after they've disappeared.'

'Thank heavens for that!' Amanda exclaimed.

'Definitely,' he agreed, then frowned. 'I'm surprised that Joanna hasn't been vaccinated against rubella, though. Isn't that one of the things they usually check on before people start their midwifery training?'

'You're right, it is, and to be fair to Joanna, she thought she had been vaccinated. However, it turns out that her parents decided not to have it done.'

'Really!' Max exclaimed. 'Why ever not?'

Amanda sighed. 'Joanna was just a baby when the combined measles, mumps and rubella vaccine was introduced. There was a lot of adverse publicity at the time and many parents were wary about letting their children have it. It seems that Joanna's parents decided not to go ahead with it too.'

'I see.' Max frowned thoughtfully. 'I wonder how many other members of staff are in the same position. It might be worth checking to make sure that everyone is immune. I can arrange for blood tests to be done after Christmas for those willing to be tested.'

'That sounds like a good idea to me,' Amanda agreed, then looked up and smiled. 'What do you think, Lucy?'

Max felt his stomach lurch when he turned and saw Lucy standing behind him. Although it was only a few days since he'd seen her, it felt as though a whole lifetime had passed. He longed to take her in his arms and feel the softness of her body nestled against him. It was only the fact that Amanda was there that stopped him, and the realisation scared him. Even though he knew how foolish it would be to get involved with her, it didn't stop him wanting her!

'I'm sorry. What did you say?' Lucy could feel her

heart hammering. She dragged her gaze away from Max, but she could feel his eyes boring into her and shivered. The past few days had been the longest of her entire life. Knowing that she wouldn't see Max over the weekend should have provided a welcome breathing space, but it hadn't turned out that way. She had missed him so much that it was hard not to show him just how pleased she was to see him.

'Max has suggested that everyone is tested to make sure they're immune to rubella,' Amanda explained. 'I think it's a good idea, don't you?'

'Yes, I do.' Lucy took a deep breath. Getting involved with Max would be a mistake. She needed time to get over what had happened with Richard and she couldn't afford to be drawn into another difficult situation. 'I'm more than happy to be tested and I'm sure everyone will feel the same.'

'Good. I'll make all the necessary arrangements, then.'

Max was all business as he turned to Amanda and asked her for an update about what else had happened while he'd been off. Lucy collected the file she needed and left them to it. With two members of staff off sick, it promised to be another busy day. Thankfully, she was working the early shift and shouldn't see very much of Max. Unless there was a crisis, then, she'd be able to avoid him.

She sighed as she made her way back to the delivery room. Although her head told her that it was a good thing, her heart definitely didn't seem to agree.

Lucy stayed on after her shift should have ended. Although Amanda had managed to find someone to cover the evening shift, she hated to leave them in the lurch, so it was gone three by the time she felt able to leave. She went to the staffroom for her coat, smiling when she found Cathy in there, nursing a mug of tea.

'You look as though you needed that.'

'Tell me about it.' Cathy took a swallow of her tea then groaned appreciatively. 'You can forget about sex. I'd rather have a mug of tea any day of the week!'

'I'm sure your boyfriend would be thrilled to hear you say that,' Lucy replied, laughing.

'Oh, Neil knows exactly how I feel,' Cathy assured her. 'We wouldn't have lasted this long if he hadn't been so understanding, believe me.'

'How long have you been together?' Lucy asked, slipping on her coat.

'Almost two years, although I've known him since we were at school together. Don't tell him I said this but I wouldn't swap him for the world, although I might just consider it if George Clooney came knocking on my door!' she added, grinning.

Lucy laughed. 'You and a million other women.'

'Hmm, good point. I don't think I'd fancy going out with a guy who dozens of other women lusted after, would you?'

'No, I wouldn't.' She didn't realise how sharp she'd sounded until she saw Cathy look at her in surprise.

'That came from the heart. Do I take it that you've had a bad experience?'

'You could say that.' Lucy shrugged. 'My ex was considered to be heart-throb material. The problem was that he knew it too.'

'Is that why you split up?' Cathy asked sympathetically.

'No. I could have coped with the female adulation. What I couldn't handle was him seeing other women while still professing his love for me.'

'Ouch!' Cathy grimaced. 'It sounds as though you had a lucky escape, if you ask me.'

'I suppose so.'

'There's no suppose about it,' Cathy said firmly, standing up. She went to her locker and took out her bag. 'What you need is to have some fun and forget about him, and I know the perfect way to do it.' She handed Lucy a ticket. 'It's the staff Christmas party tonight. I was supposed to be going with Joanna but obviously she won't be able to make it now, so you can have her ticket.'

'Oh, I don't know if I should,' Lucy began.

'Rubbish! Of course you should! It'll be fun, trust me. And you never know, you might meet someone who'll take your mind right off your ex!'

Lucy laughed as she took the ticket. However, as she left the staffroom she couldn't help thinking that it wasn't Richard who had occupied her thoughts recently. She sighed. She had a feeling that it was going to take more than a few hours of fun to stop her thinking about Max all the time.

CHAPTER NINE

MAX wasn't planning on going to the Christmas party, even though he had bought a ticket months ago. After his last disastrous date, he had given up on the idea of socialising for the moment. However, as the day wore on, the prospect of spending the evening on his own held even less appeal. He knew what would happen. He would spend the time thinking about Lucy and it wouldn't help one little bit. The Christmas party could turn out to be the better option.

He went home to shower and change then drove back to the hospital. The party was being held in the staff canteen and there was quite a crowd in there when he arrived. He got himself a drink from the makeshift bar and went to find the others, stopping en route to speak to various people he knew. Everyone was in high spirits and he only wished he felt as cheerful as they did. However, he was suddenly very conscious of the fact that this would be the last Christmas he spent in Dalverston and the thought weighed heavily on him. It was hard to appear his usual happy-go-lucky self when he joined the staff from the maternity unit.

'We didn't know you were coming, Max!' Anita Walsh exclaimed. 'You should have said and then we could have picked you up in the minibus to save you driving.'

'I wasn't sure if I could make it,' he hedged, not wanting to explain why it had been a last-minute decision. He held up his glass, wanting to deflect any more awkward questions. 'OK, guys, I'd like to propose a toast. To everyone who works on the maternity unit. May we all enjoy the fruits of other people's labours!'

Everyone laughed as they clinked glasses. Max was relieved that he had managed to divert attention away from himself. There were several former members of staff there that night and he decided to have word with them. If he kept circulating, hopefully no one would notice that he wasn't his usual ebullient self.

He was just heading over to speak to Maria, who had retired recently, when he saw Lucy crossing the canteen and his heart seemed to leap right up into his throat. He'd had no idea that she would be there that night. Tickets had sold out months ago, long before she had moved to Dalverston. Now the shock of seeing her so unexpectedly turned his limbs to stone. He could only stand and stare as she drew closer.

Lucy felt shock scud through her when she spotted Max. She'd never dreamt that he would be there that night and wasn't sure what she should do. She paused, wondering if she should beat a hasty retreat, but just at that moment Cathy spotted her.

'There you are!' Cathy exclaimed as she came hurrying over to her. 'I thought you must have changed your mind and decided not to come after all.'

'I…um…I'm sorry I'm late but the bus didn't turn up so I had to find a taxi.'

'I should have asked you if you wanted to come in

the minibus,' Cathy said apologetically. 'I never gave it a thought. Sorry.'

'It doesn't matter,' Lucy said quickly. She shot a glance at Max and felt herself colour when she realised that he was watching her. Her heart seemed to be beating at double its normal speed when she turned to Cathy again. 'I'm here now and that's the main thing.'

'Of course it is.' Cathy grinned as she led her over to the rest of their group and raised her glass aloft. 'OK, folks, now it's my turn to propose a toast. Here's to a fun-filled night!'

Everyone cheered as they raised their glasses. Lucy joined in but she was so conscious of Max that it was hard to act naturally. She shot another glance in his direction and was relieved to see that he was talking to a glamorous older woman and no longer looking at her. She made her way to the far side of the group, wondering how soon she could leave without it causing comment. Being around Max was the last thing she needed at the present time.

Someone put some music on and people started to dance. When Cathy urged everyone to join in, Lucy went willingly. With a bit of luck she'd be able to slip away while they were occupied. Max was dancing with the other woman now, laughing as he guided her around the floor in a stately waltz. They passed Lucy and she blushed when he caught her staring and winked at her.

The first track ended and another one began. It was a popular tune and more people came onto the floor. Lucy doubted if anyone would notice her leaving in all the crush so started to edge towards the door, only to stop when Adam Sanders came over and asked her to dance.

There was no way she could refuse without it appearing rude, so she followed him back to the floor. Max was dancing with Cathy now. Lucy could hear her laughing at something he was saying but looked the other way in case he thought she was watching him again. One dance led to a second before she was able to excuse herself, ignoring Adam's obvious disappointment. She sighed as she made her way towards the exit. Adam was very nice but she just wasn't interested in him.

'Will you dance with me, Lucy?'

All of a sudden Max appeared at her side and she stopped dead. 'Dance with you,' she repeated numbly.

'Uhuh.' He placed his hand on his heart and grinned at her. 'I promise on my honour that I'll do my very best not to trample all over your toes.'

Lucy's mouth quirked before she could stop it. 'That doesn't sound very encouraging. Just how bad a dancer are you?'

'You'll have to judge for yourself.' He smiled as he held out his hand. 'Come on, Lucy. Take pity on me. If you won't dance with me then I'll be left standing here like a wallflower!'

'I don't think so. I imagine you could find yourself another partner easily enough.'

'Maybe. But it's you I want to dance with, so won't you say yes? Please?'

Lucy felt her stomach muscles clench when she saw the expression in his eyes. She knew she should refuse but it was impossible when he looked at her so beseechingly. She placed her hand in his and let him lead her back to the floor. There was a fast number playing this time and everyone was having a wonderful time. Max laughed as he swung her round to face him.

'I hope you're ready for this.'

'Bring it on,' she assured him, and he chuckled.

'Well, you only have yourself to blame.'

He spun her round, twisting her this way and that until she was breathless. Despite what he had said, he was an excellent dancer and she glowered at him when the music came to an end.

'There's absolutely nothing wrong with the way you dance!'

'That's all down to you.' He smiled at her. 'I've raised my game to keep up with my partner.'

'I don't think so!' she scoffed. 'If you ask me, insinuating that you're a rubbish dancer is just a line. I expect a lot of women fall for it, don't they, Max?'

'If it helped to persuade you to dance with me, that's all that matters,' he said quietly.

Lucy felt heat flash through her veins when he pulled her into his arms. The music had changed to a slow tune now and when the lights were dimmed, she closed her eyes, giving herself up to the seductive rhythm. She could feel his lips nuzzling her hair and sighed, enjoying the feeling of closeness and the fact that it made her feel special to be held like this, desired.

'I could dance with you like this for ever, Lucy.'

Lucy frowned when she heard the grating note in his voice. Bearing in mind what he had said about not wanting a long-term relationship, it seemed very strange. Opening her eyes, she tipped back her head and looked at him. 'I thought you avoided commitment?'

'I do. But it doesn't mean that I don't have feelings.'

He drew her to him so that she could feel his arousal pressing against her. Lucy swallowed when she felt her nipples immediately peak in response. She was wearing a black silk dress that night and she knew that Max could tell she was aroused too.

He drew her even closer, his fingers splaying across the base of her spine as they swayed together in time to the music. Lucy could feel the tension growing with each second that passed and shivered. It was obvious that Max wanted her and it made her wonder why he'd been so keen to call a halt when he had. Surely it would have made more sense if he'd tried to persuade her to have an affair with him?

She was still trying to puzzle it out when the music stopped and the lights came up. She stepped out of his arms, feeling light-headed and giddy as the thoughts whizzed around her head. Leaving aside Max's motives, what would *she* have said if he had tried to talk her into having an affair? It was easy to claim that she would have refused but was that really true? Although she knew that Max was the last person she should get involved with, there was no point pretending that she didn't want him. But was it purely lust she felt, or something more? She wished she knew because maybe then she would know what to do about it.

Max could barely think thanks to the flood of emotions that filled his mind as well as his body. He had never felt this strongly about any woman and the thought scared him half to death. He knew that he needed to get a grip on himself but it was proving harder than he'd expected to do that.

'Come on, you two, get a move on. The buffet's being served and all the food will be gone if we don't get there pronto.'

Max jumped when Cathy tapped him on the shoulder.

He summoned a smile, but it was hard to disguise how worried he felt. 'I'm not hungry, thanks. I think I'll pass.'

'All the more for the rest of us,' Cathy quipped. 'What about you, Lucy?'

'I'll get something in a minute, thanks.'

Lucy smiled at the other woman but Max could tell the effort it cost her and his heart seemed to scrunch up inside him. Lucy was obviously finding it as difficult as he was to deal with this situation, and that was even more worrying. He turned to her as Cathy moved away to badger someone else.

'Are you all right?'

'I'm fine, thank you.'

When he heard the wobble in her voice, Max was hard pressed not to haul her back into his arms and to hell with the consequences, only he knew that he couldn't do that. It wouldn't be fair to her or to himself to let this situation develop any further. Lucy deserved so much more than he could ever give her. She deserved a man who could give her children, and he wasn't that man. He couldn't bear to think that one day she could come to hate him, couldn't stand the thought that his shortcomings as a man would come back to haunt him once again.

The pain he felt was so sharp, so intense, that he could barely stand it. He knew that he had to leave before he ended up making a fool of himself. When Amanda came over to speak to them, he quietly excused himself. Most people were queuing up for the buffet and nobody noticed him leaving, so he was able to make his escape without it causing a fuss.

He sighed as he left the hospital and headed over to

his car. So much for hoping the party would take his mind off Lucy! All it had done was to make him see how impossible the situation was. The sooner he left Dalverston the better. Lucy could get on with her life and he could get on with his.

Lucy had the following two days off and spent them catching up with any jobs that needed doing. Although her flat was tiny, she spent a long time making sure everywhere was clean and tidy. She knew that she was keeping busy for the sake of it but it was the only way she could cope with what had happened between her and Max.

The fact that he had left the party without saying goodbye to her had hurt. There had seemed to be a real connection between them that night, yet he had walked away without a word. She couldn't help feeling let down even though she knew it was foolish. Max didn't do commitment and she didn't want him to, so why did she feel so upset?

By the time she went into work on Christmas Eve, Lucy felt more confused than ever. It didn't help that the unit was almost deserted when she arrived. With no new admissions that day, most of the staff had been sent home early. Even the wards were eerily quiet as the majority of patients had been discharged.

'It's like the *Marie Celeste* in here,' she observed when she went into the office for the handover.

'Don't knock it!' Tina Marshall, one of their part-time staff who was working that night, admonished her. 'I, for one, will be perfectly happy if it stays like this. I've got three children who are bouncing off the walls with excitement, waiting for Father Christmas to arrive.

I doubt if I'll get any sleep when I get home in the morning, so the quieter it is tonight, the happier I'll be.'

'Thank heavens my lot are past that stage,' Amanda declared. She quickly updated them about the remaining patients in the wards and then stood up. 'That's it, then. Diane's gone to the canteen for her break, but she should be back soon. Oh, and the staff choir will be doing their rounds at some point, singing Christmas carols. You'll never guess who's playing Father Christmas this year.'

'Why? Who is it?' Lucy demanded, but Amanda just grinned.

'Wait and see!'

No amount of pleading would make her tell them so in the end they gave up. Lucy went to the desk after Amanda had left. There was a stack of notes belonging to the patients who had been discharged that day that needed filing so she took them into the office and set to work. It didn't take her very long to finish the job and she was just wondering what she should do next when she heard voices in the corridor.

She hurried to the door and gasped when she saw a group of people gathered around the desk. They were dressed in an assortment of costumes ranging from elves and fairies to sheep. Father Christmas cut a fine figure in his flowing red robes, although she had no idea who was beneath the bushy white beard until he spoke.

'Ho, ho, ho. A merry Christmas to you, young lady,' Max said in an exaggeratedly deep voice that made her want to giggle.

'And a merry Christmas to you, too, Santa,' she replied, almost choking on her laughter.

'We've come to spread a little Christmas cheer,' he

informed her. He handed her a song sheet. 'Everyone's welcome to join in, elves, fairies, staff and patients.'

'Thank you.'

Lucy smiled as she took the sheet from him and he smiled back. Just for a second his eyes held hers and she felt her heart leap when she saw the awareness they held. She was immediately transported back to when he had held her in his arms at the Christmas party. There *had* been a connection between them that night, just as there was a connection between them now. Maybe it wasn't what either of them wanted but there was no point trying to deny it.

It was all very unsettling. When the choir began to sing the first carol, Lucy found it hard to concentrate. However, the familiar strains of 'Away in a Manger' soon had her singing along. They went into the wards where Max handed out fluffy white teddy bears to all the babies. He had a word with each of the mums and she couldn't help noticing how they all responded to him. It wasn't just the fact that Max was a very attractive man but that he obviously cared about people, and they responded to that. Once again she found herself thinking how at odds his attitude was to the way he lived his life.

They left the wards and made their way to the special care baby unit where Max placed a teddy on every incubator. When the choir began to sing 'Silent Night', Lucy wasn't the only one with tears in her eyes. There was something incredibly moving about hearing the beautiful old carol sung in a place where the most vulnerable babies were cared for.

'That was really lovely,' she said sincerely as they left SCBU.

'It always leaves a lump in my throat,' Max admitted as he followed her along the corridor.

'Me too. So where are you off to next?' she asked, pausing when they came to the stairs.

'There's just Women's Surgical left to do and that's it. I can hang up my robe and beard. I must say that I won't be sorry to part with the latter. It's incredibly hot and itchy!'

Lucy laughed when he began to scratch his chin. 'Good job you won't have to wear it for very much longer. Do you usually play Father Christmas?'

'No, this is a first for me. Sam Kearney was supposed to be doing it this year but he got held up in Resus. He phoned me to ask if I'd take over for him and I couldn't think of a way to refuse.'

'Well, I'm sure everyone appreciated your efforts.'

'Let's hope so.' He gave her a quick smile then went to catch up with the rest of the party.

Lucy went back to the office, wishing that she could have thought of something to keep him there a bit longer. She sighed because it was dangerous to think like that. She needed to stay away from Max instead of concocting reasons to be with him. She found the laundry list and went to put away the fresh supplies that had been delivered. Tina helped her and they had just finished when the phone rang.

'I'll get it,' Lucy said, hurrying to the desk. 'Maternity. Lucy Harris speaking.'

It was Helen Roberts's husband, phoning to tell them that Helen had gone into labour. He sounded frantic with worry and Lucy understood why when he explained that he had phoned for an ambulance only to be told that it could be some time before one reached them.

Apparently, there'd been a serious accident on the motorway and every available ambulance had been deployed there. With his leg still in a cast, Martin was unable to drive Helen to the hospital himself.

'Is there anyone else who could drive her here?' Lucy asked.

'No, nobody. Mum and Dad are away on a cruise and they won't be back for another week,' Martin told her anxiously.

'How about a neighbour, perhaps?'

'Jack Walsh is our nearest neighbour—he lives about ten miles away,' Martin informed her. 'I know it doesn't sound very far, but we've had a lot of snow in the past few days and the roads are virtually impassable in places. It could take an hour or more for Jack to get here.'

'That's probably as long as it would take an ambulance to get to you,' Lucy said, trying not to show how concerned she felt. She knew how dangerous it would be for Helen to give birth without the necessary precautions being taken. Poor glycaemic control during labour and birth could affect the baby, causing respiratory distress and hypoglycaemia amongst other things. Helen would need either insulin injections or intravenous dextrose plus insulin to keep her stable. She realised that she needed to discuss the situation with someone else.

'I need to speak to one of the doctors about this, Martin, so I'm going to have to phone you back.'

'You won't be long, will you? We really need help here asap.'

'I'll be as quick as I can,' she assured him. She hung up then contacted the switchboard and asked them to page Diane, quickly explaining what had happened as soon as the registrar phoned her back.

'I don't know what to suggest,' Diane admitted worriedly. 'Obviously, the situation is extremely urgent but without an ambulance to ferry Helen here, I don't know what we can do. I'll give Max a call and see what he says.'

Lucy hung up, checking her watch to see how much time had elapsed. Although the conversation had taken only a few minutes, every second counted. When the phone rang, she snatched up the receiver. 'What did Max say?'

There was a tiny pause before Max's voice came down the line. 'Diane just told me what's happened. I've spoken to Ambulance Control and they're trying to organise an ambulance, but it could take some time to get one out to the farm.'

'What about the neighbouring authorities?' she suggested, trying to still the thunderous beating of her heart, but hearing his voice so unexpectedly had thrown her off balance. 'Can they help?'

'Apparently they've already deployed any spare ambulances to the RTA. Ambulance Control will have to try further afield, possibly Lancaster or Penrith.'

'But they're miles away from here!'

'I know. I'm not happy about it either, but it's the best they can do in the circumstances. In the meantime, I'm going to drive up to the farm myself. I was on my way home when Diane phoned me but it won't take me long to get back to the unit and collect what I need.'

He paused and Lucy realised that she was holding her breath as she waited for him to continue. 'The thing is that I need someone to go with me. I've had a word with

Carol Jackson, the nursing manager, and she's agreed
to find cover. A couple of the community midwives are
on standby and I'm sure one of them will come in if it's
necessary. So will you come with me, Lucy? Please.'

CHAPTER TEN

'How much further is it now?'

Max changed down a gear, keeping his gaze locked on the increasingly treacherous surface of the road. Thick snow blanketed the surrounding countryside, with drifts several feet deep in places. He couldn't imagine how an ambulance would manage to negotiate these roads in such appalling conditions, which made it all the more imperative that they get through.

'A couple of miles.' Lucy angled the light from the torch so that she could see the map. 'There should be a turning down here on the left any second now... There it is!'

Max slowed the car to a crawl before he turned into the lane. Even so, he felt the rear end slide sideways and held his breath as he steered into the skid. The last thing they needed was to end up in a ditch!

'I'm glad I'm not driving.' Lucy grimaced as the car righted itself and they set off down the lane. 'It's horrendously slippy.'

'It is. I can't see an ambulance making it up here, can you?' Max observed, resisting the urge to look at her. He needed to keep his attention on the road, he reminded himself, then sighed. Just sitting next to Lucy was distracting enough.

'No, I can't. So what are we going to do if we can't get Helen to the hospital before the baby arrives?'

She sounded worried and he hurried to reassure her. 'Exactly what we would do if Helen was in the unit. We have everything we need, Lucy—insulin, dextrose, pain relief, the lot.'

'And what if she needs a section? I mean, it could happen, Max. I know the recent scans of the baby seemed fine but….'

'But nothing. We'll deal with that if and when it happens.' He reached over and squeezed her hand. 'Don't go borrowing trouble, as my granny used to say.'

She gave a shaky laugh as she withdrew her hand. 'Your granny sounds like a very wise woman.'

She busied herself with the map, making it clear that she didn't want any more reassurances. Max gripped the steering-wheel, feeling his fingers tingling from the brief contact they'd made with hers. Could Lucy feel it too, he wondered, feel those frissons of awareness flickering under her skin? He thought she did, and it only made him feel even more conscious of her sitting beside him. To know that Lucy shared these feelings he had was both a torment and a joy.

It was another ten minutes before they finally reached the farmhouse. Max heaved a sigh of relief as he switched off the engine. 'I didn't think we were going to make it down that last stretch. The snow was so thick that the tyres couldn't get a grip.'

'I'm glad it's over,' Lucy said thankfully, opening the car door. She hurried round to the back and opened the tailgate, reaching for the box of supplies they'd brought with them.

'I'll take that if you'll carry my case,' Max told her,

lifting the box out of the Land Rover. They headed to the house and Lucy knocked on the door. Martin opened it and it was obvious how relieved he was to see them.

'Thanks heavens you made it!' He ushered them into the kitchen, using one of his crutches to direct them along the hall. 'Through there on your left. Helen's in the sitting room. We've been sleeping downstairs—it's easier than negotiating the stairs with these things.'

'We'll find her,' Max assured him. He led the way to the sitting room and found Helen lying on the sofa. 'How are you doing?'

'Not too bad.' She summoned a smile but Max could see the worry in her eyes. 'It's the baby I'm more concerned about. If my glucose levels aren't right then it could cause problems when it's born, couldn't it?'

'Yes, it could, but that isn't going to happen, Helen. We're going to keep a close watch on your blood glucose levels, aren't we, Lucy?' He turned to Lucy, trying to ignore the flood of emotions that filled him. He didn't have time to worry about how he felt when he needed to concentrate on Helen and her baby.

'We are. In fact, we shall do everything exactly the same as we would have done if you'd been in hospital,' she confirmed, using his own words to reassure Helen. They obviously worked because Helen's smile was less forced this time.

'Thank you. That's good to hear.'

The next half-hour flew past. After he had checked Helen's blood glucose levels, Lucy helped him set up the drip. The mixture of dextrose and insulin would help to maintain Helen's glucose levels during the birth, although they would need to monitor the situation very closely. The sofa pulled out into a double bed, so once

Martin had told them where to find clean sheets and blankets, they got that ready as well.

Max had brought a portable foetal monitor with him and as soon as Helen was comfortably settled, he checked the baby's heart rate and was relieved to find that it appeared perfectly normal. Although he knew they were doing everything possible to ensure both the mother's and the child's safety, he would feel a lot happier once they got Helen to hospital.

He excused himself and went into the hall to phone the ambulance control centre for an update. It wasn't good news and it was hard to hide his concern when he went back to the sitting room. Lucy obviously realised something was amiss because she came hurrying over to him.

'What's happened?' she said quietly so Helen and Martin couldn't hear her.

'Apparently, an ambulance was dispatched half an hour ago. Ambulance Control has just received a message to say that it's stuck in the snow and the crew don't think they'll be able to go any further. They've been told to return to base once they've dug themselves out.'

'So what's going to happen now?'

'I've asked them to get onto the air ambulance service and see if they can help. If we can get a helicopter out here, that will solve our problems.'

'Will it be able to fly in these conditions, though?'

'I really don't know. All we can do is cross our fingers and hope we get a break. Anyway, how's Helen doing?' he asked, refusing to dwell on what they would do if the helicopter failed to reach them.

'Her contractions are speeding up.' Lucy took her cue from him. Her voice held no trace of the anxiety he knew she must be feeling. Max couldn't help feeling proud of the way she was responding to the challenge but deemed it wiser not to say anything. He couldn't afford to let his emotions get in the way of him doing his job.

'Is she fully dilated?'

'Not yet. She's about eight centimetres so we've a bit of time yet. Is there anything in particular that I need to look out for when the baby is born?'

'We'll start with the usual assessment and carry on from there. There's been no indication that Helen's baby is suffering from congenital heart problems, but obviously we need to be aware of that,' Max explained. 'Hypoglycaemia can be an issue, so a blood glucose test will need to be done two to four hours after the birth, which is another reason why we need to get the baby to hospital as soon as possible. Other tests will be carried out if there are any clinical signs to indicate that there's a problem.'

'It's better if the baby feeds as soon as possible, isn't it?' Lucy clarified.

'Yes. Within thirty minutes of the birth is recommended, then every two to three hours after that until feeding maintains pre-feed blood glucose levels at a minimum of 2.0 mmol/litre.'

'And if it drops below that level?'

'If it happens on two consecutive readings, the baby will need to be fed by tube or given intravenous dextrose. However, I'm hoping neither of those will be necessary and definitely not while we're here.'

'Amen to that,' Lucy agreed fervently.

'It's going to be fine,' Max assured her. 'All we

have to do is hold the fort until the air ambulance gets here.'

'As simple as that, eh?' she said, rolling her eyes. 'We sit tight until the cavalry arrives.'

Max laughed. 'That's it. Easy-peasy, as my niece Emily would say.'

Lucy looked at him curiously. 'I didn't have you down as a doting uncle.'

'No?' He shrugged. 'My brothers have five children between them, so I've well earned my stripes.'

'You like children, then?'

'Of course I do. Why wouldn't I?'

'Oh, no reason.'

She gave him a quick smile and moved away. Max sighed as he watched her go over to Helen. Lucy obviously thought that his bachelor status was a sign that he wasn't keen on children and that couldn't be further from the truth. Just for a second he longed to explain the situation to her before he realised how pointless it was. Lucy wasn't going to play any part in his future, so it wouldn't make a scrap of difference to her if he couldn't have kids.

Lucy made a note of Helen's blood pressure then glanced at the clock. Twenty minutes had passed since Max had spoken to the ambulance control centre. Was the helicopter on its way, or had the crew decided that the weather conditions were too bad for them to risk flying? She had no idea what they were going to do if it failed to arrive. All they could do was sit tight and hope that help would arrive eventually.

She frowned as she unfastened the cuff from around Helen's arm because that thought had reminded her of what Max had told her. In her experience, men like him, who enjoyed such a hedonistic lifestyle, weren't usually interested in other people's children. However, there'd been genuine affection in his voice when he had spoken about his niece and it was yet another factor that didn't add up.

'I'll get onto Ambulance Control again and see what's happening.'

Lucy glanced round when Max suddenly appeared at her side. 'Good idea. We need to know if that helicopter is on its way,' she agreed, hoping he couldn't hear the uncertainty in her voice. She'd made one massive error of judgement with Richard and she would be a fool to make another one now. She should accept the situation for what it was and stop trying to justify Max's behaviour all the time.

'Fingers crossed,' he murmured, heading for the door.

Lucy put the sphygmomanometer back in its case then checked the drip. Although Helen's contractions were strong, she still wasn't fully dilated. It would be a while yet before the baby was born, which meant there was still time to get her to hospital if the helicopter arrived soon.

'No sign of that helicopter yet?' Martin asked anxiously.

'Max is phoning ambulance control for an update,' Lucy explained as calmly as she could because it wouldn't help if she appeared worried as well.

'I should have insisted that you went to stay at your mother's,' Martin said, turning to glare at his wife. 'There wouldn't have been a problem if you'd been in town.'

'And how would you have managed here on your own, with your leg in plaster?' Helen retorted.

'I'd have coped well enough,' Martin said gruffly. 'Anyway, Bert would have given me a hand if I'd needed it.'

Helen rolled her eyes as she turned to Lucy. 'Bert's our stockman and the most curmudgeonly old devil you can imagine. I don't think he's said more than a dozen words to either of us since Martin took over the farm after his father retired. Somehow, I can't picture Bert playing nursemaid!'

She broke off when another contraction began. Lucy smiled to herself when she saw Martin lean over and rub Helen's back. Despite their disagreement, it was obvious how they felt about each other. They had the kind of close and loving relationship she had always dreamed about, a relationship that grew stronger with time. With a sudden flash of insight she realised that her relationship with Richard would never have been like that, even if it had survived. It took selflessness to put the other person first, to find happiness by making them happy, and Richard wasn't capable of that. He always put his needs before everyone else's and was only truly happy if he was getting what *he* wanted.

In her heart, Lucy had known that but she had chosen to ignore her doubts. She had been as much at fault as Richard had in a way because she had deliberately deceived herself, and that was something she must never do again. She looked up when the door opened as Max came back, and felt her pulse begin to race. If she was to be truthful about her feelings from now on then she couldn't lie about the way she felt about Max. It would be only too easy to fall in love with him, even if it would be a mistake.

'The helicopter's on its way. It was ferrying another

casualty to Penrith, which is why there's been a delay, but it should be here in roughly ten minutes' time.' Max frowned when the information was met with silence. 'Did you hear what I said, Lucy? The helicopter's on its way.'

'I…um…yes. That's brilliant news.'

She gave him a bright smile but he could tell how forced it was. If he hadn't needed to prepare for the helicopter's arrival, he would have demanded to know what was wrong, but he simply didn't have the time to spare.

'We need to find a place where it can land,' he explained, turning to Martin. 'Obviously, it has to be flat and well away from any trees or overhead cables that could snag the rotors.'

'The field behind the house is the best place,' Martin said immediately.

'Great. Can you show me where it is…? Oh, and have you got any torches or anything similar which we can use to guide them in?'

'Sure. I've a stack of lanterns in the barn, we can use them.'

Martin grabbed his crutches and hurriedly left the room. Max followed him, leaving it to Lucy to get Helen ready for the transfer. He sighed as he followed Martin across the farmyard. Maybe it was a good thing that he hadn't tried to find out what was troubling her. He was already in far deeper than he should have been and he needed to keep his distance, even if it was proving extremely difficult to do so. He just had to remember that he was doing this for her sake as well as his and hope that it would help.

* * *

The flight to the hospital was extremely bumpy. A strong wind had sprung up, threatening to blow them off course at one point. Lucy heaved a sigh of relief when the helicopter touched down safely on the landing pad on the hospital's roof. As soon as the blades stopped spinning, Helen was lifted onto a trolley and rushed inside. Lucy hurried along beside her. Max had stopped to thank the crew but he soon caught up with them.

'I want you to check her blood glucose levels as soon as we get her into the delivery room. The stress could have had an adverse effect.'

'Right.' Lucy hurried on ahead, automatically checking the board behind the desk to see which rooms were vacant. She was surprised to discover that two suites were occupied.

'It looks as though it's been busier than we expected,' she said, elbowing open the door to suite number three. 'Tina must have been run off her feet.'

'I'll check everything's OK once we've got Helen settled,' Max told her. He helped the porters line up the trolley beside the bed so that Helen could slide across, then attached her to the foetal monitor. He smiled when the baby's heartbeat echoed around the room. 'Well, this little fellow seems happy enough. He obviously enjoyed his first ride in a helicopter.'

'I just wish Martin had been able to come with us,' Helen said, her voice catching. There'd been no room for Martin in the helicopter so they'd had to leave him behind. 'He desperately wanted to be at the birth and now he's going to miss it.'

'There's still time for him to get here,' Lucy assured her, mentally crossing her fingers. 'It could be a while yet before your baby is born, so if he can get someone to drive him here he might make it in time.'

She knew it was a long shot, but if it stopped Helen fretting that was the main thing. Max gave her a quick smile as she set about checking Helen's glucose levels and her heart lifted. Even though she knew how dangerous it was, it felt good to know that she had earned his approval.

CHAPTER ELEVEN

HELEN's baby was born at four fifty-five on Christmas morning. True to his word, Martin was there for the birth. A neighbour had driven him to the hospital on his quad bike and he was covered in snow when he arrived. Lucy laughed when Trish ushered him into the room.

'You look like the abominable snowman!'

'I feel like it,' Martin declared, stripping off his jacket. He dumped it on the floor in the corner then hobbled over to the bed and smiled at his wife. 'I told you I'd be here, didn't I?'

'You did.' Helen smiled as she took hold of his hand and held it tightly. 'Although if you'd left it any later you'd have missed the main event!'

Everyone laughed before they concentrated on what needed doing. The baby's head had crowned and a few seconds later it emerged. After another few contractions, first one shoulder and then the other were delivered before the rest of the body slid out. Lucy quickly wiped away the mucus from the baby's mouth and held him so that his head was lower than his body. He hadn't breathed yet so she blew hard on his chest then tapped the soles of his feet when he still didn't respond. Max was tying and cutting the cord and as soon as he'd finished, she carried the baby over to the table, using a length of narrow tubing to clear any remaining mucus from his airway then massaged his chest and back with a towel. However, he still didn't make any attempt to breathe.

'What's wrong?' Helen demanded. 'Why isn't he crying?'

Lucy was too busy to answer and left it to Max to explain that they needed to start artificial respiration. Using a small-sized bag, she puffed air into the baby's lungs, watching as the tiny chest rose. Max came to join her and she saw the worry on his face when he checked for a pulse.

'Heart's stopped beating.'

Lucy nodded, not needing him to explain what they had to do next. She puffed some more air into the baby's lungs then watched as Max used the tip of his index finger to gently press on the baby's chest and massage his heart. The method for resuscitating a baby was basically the same as that used to resuscitate an adult. The difference was that one needed to be extremely gentle.

They repeated the process several times before Max held up his hand. 'Wait a moment... Yes! His heart's beating. Come on, little fellow, how about a nice big breath for your uncle Max?'

As though he had understood, the baby suddenly took his first breath. Lucy smiled in delight when he let out a loud wail. 'That's it. Have a good scream and let everyone know that you're not happy about being poked and prodded.'

Max chuckled as he watched the baby's face change from a waxy white to an angry red colour. 'I think he's taking you at your word. There's definitely nothing wrong with his lungs, from the sound of it.'

'There certainly isn't,' Lucy agreed. She wrapped the baby in a warm blanket and carried him over to his anxious parents. 'Here you go. One very grumpy little boy who needs some TLC from his mum and dad.'

'Thank you so much.' Tears were streaming down Helen's cheeks as she cradled her son in her arms. 'I was so scared when he didn't cry…'

She broke off, overcome with emotion. Lucy patted her hand, understanding how terrifying it must have been for her. 'He's fine now and that's the main thing.'

'Was it because of Helen's diabetes?' Martin asked in a choked voice. 'Was that why he couldn't breathe on his own at first?'

'Not at all. Some babies just need a little encouragement before they take their first breath,' Max assured him, playing down the drama of what had happened.

'But his heart wasn't beating either,' Helen put in. She bit her lip. 'Does it mean there's something wrong with him—with his heart, I mean?'

'Obviously, we can't rule it out until we've done some tests. All I can say is that none of the scans you had indicated that there's a problem.' His tone was gentle. 'I know it's difficult, Helen, but try not to worry. You won't do yourself any good if you get worked up.'

'I'll try,' Helen assured him. She dropped a kiss on her son's head then smiled at her husband. 'He's beautiful, isn't he?'

Lucy moved away from the bed as the couple set about the age-old ritual of counting their child's fingers and toes. They were such lovely people and she only hoped that nothing would show up in the tests to spoil their delight at becoming parents. She gave them a few minutes on their own then went back and explained that the baby needed to be fed. She knew that Helen was keen to breastfeed so she helped her get comfortable and showed her how to hold her son so that he was in the best position. They all laughed when he immediately began suckling greedily.

By the time she went off duty, Lucy was much more hopeful that everything would be fine. Max had arranged for an echocardiograph to be done as well as a range of other tests, but with a bit of luck nothing untoward would show up. As she went to fetch her coat, she couldn't help thinking how well everything had turned out after such a traumatic start. Diane was in the staffroom when Lucy went in and she grinned at her.

'I bet you're ready for home after the night you've had.'

'It was a bit hairy at times,' she agreed. 'How did you get on? I was surprised when I saw that there'd been two more admissions.'

'One of them has gone home,' Diane told her. 'Turned out it was a false alarm so she decided not to stay. The other is still in the delivery room. It could be a while yet before the baby arrives so it looks as though you've won this year's competition.'

'What competition?' Lucy asked in surprise.

'The midwife who delivers the first Christmas Day baby wins a bottle of champagne,' Diane explained.

'Really?'

'Yes. I don't know who started it but it's become a bit of a tradition around here. The consultant pays for it so it looks as though Max will have to cough up this year. Make sure you remind him.'

'Oh, right. Yes, of course,' Lucy agreed, knowing full well that she had no intention of doing so. Although it was a nice gesture, she would feel extremely uncomfortable about demanding that Max should buy her a bottle of champagne and even more uneasy at the thought of them sharing it!

Heat rose to her face and she hurriedly closed her locker. She didn't intend to go down that route, certainly didn't want to picture them clinking glasses and staring into one another's eyes. 'I'll get off, then. Are you working tonight?'

'Yes, unfortunately.' Diane grimaced as she wound her scarf around her neck. 'My boyfriend's not at all happy about it either. He's done nothing but grumble ever since I told him I had to work over Christmas. I wouldn't mind, but it's not as though we actually do anything. Christmas is usually spent vegging out in front of the television!'

'You're not alone,' Lucy laughed. 'That's what most folk do.'

'I suppose so.' Diane laughed. 'I know I shouldn't complain. At least it proves that he misses me when I'm at work…or I *think* it does.'

Lucy was still laughing as they left the staffroom. They waved goodbye to the day staff and headed to the lifts. The night shift was going off duty and they had to wait a couple of minutes for the lift to arrive. Lucy felt her heart jolt when the doors opened and Max stepped out. He smiled when he saw her.

'I'm glad I caught you. I just wanted to let you know that everything is looking very positive for Helen's baby. The echocardiograph is clear and his blood glucose levels are stable.'

'That's wonderful news. Have you told Helen and Martin yet?'

'No. I'm on way to do it now. Anyway, I won't keep you. I'm sure you're looking forward to getting home.'

He started to turn away but just then Diane piped up. 'Don't forget that you owe Lucy a bottle of champagne, Max.'

'Do I?' He glanced back, a frown drawing his brows together. Lucy could feel the colour rushing to her cheeks again as the images she had tried to dispel earlier came flooding back. Max's eyes would be so deep and intent as they stared into hers…

She took a quick breath to chase away the pictures, wishing with all her heart that Diane hadn't said anything. However, it seemed the registrar was determined that Lucy should receive her prize.

'Yes. The midwife who delivers the first baby born on Christmas Day wins a bottle of champagne, Max. You must know that.'

'Of course. Sorry, I'd forgotten all about it.' He turned to Lucy and shrugged. 'I'll sort it out as soon as I can if that's OK with you.'

'It's fine. Really. Don't worry about it,' she said, quickly stepping into the lift. The doors glided shut and she breathed a sigh of relief. With a bit of luck Max would forget all about it.

It was almost eight a.m. by the time Max arrived home that morning. Having left his car at the farm, he'd had to beg a lift and that had delayed him. As he let himself into his flat, he could feel weariness washing over him. He had been on the go for almost twenty-four hours and what he needed now was a long, hot shower followed by several hours of uninterrupted sleep.

The shower was soon accomplished; however, by the time he got into bed, he discovered that he no longer felt sleepy. He closed his eyes and tried to relax, but sleep eluded him. He kept thinking about what had happened the night before. It was as though everything he and Lucy had done was imprinted in his mind and he kept going over and over it, remembering what she'd said and how she'd looked until he thought he would go crazy. He knew that he couldn't allow himself to get so hung up on her, yet he couldn't seem to stop it.

In the end he got up and dressed rather than lie there any longer, torturing himself. He made himself a pot of coffee then phoned his brother Simon and told him that he wouldn't be able to make it for Christmas dinner seeing as he didn't have any transport. Simon immediately offered to drive over to collect him but Max refused. Apart from not wanting to ruin his brother's day, he didn't feel like socialising.

He finished his coffee then wandered around the flat, wondering what to do with himself. What he needed was a distraction, something to take his mind off Lucy and this situation he was in. In the end, he decided to go for a walk. Although it was bitterly cold outside, at least the icy air should help to clear his head.

Max followed the roads without any particular destination in mind. It wasn't until he found himself outside Lucy's flat that he realised he'd been heading in that direction all along. Even though he knew it was madness he needed to see her, talk to her, just *be* with her. It was like an addiction and he couldn't fight it any longer.

Taking a deep breath, he rang the bell.

* * *

Lucy had just stepped out of the shower when the door-bell rang. She frowned as she fastened the belt on her robe, because she certainly wasn't expecting any visitors. She was tempted to ignore it until it occurred to her that maybe the caller was here to see one of the other tenants and had rung her bell by mistake.

She ran downstairs and opened the front door, feeling the blood drain from her head when she found Max standing on the step. He gave her a crooked grin as he took stock of what she was wearing.

'Happy Christmas. I hope I didn't wake you up.'

'No. I'd just got out of the shower when you rang the bell.' She took a quick breath, struggling to contain the rush of emotions that were flooding through her. Although she had no idea what he wanted, she couldn't pretend that she wasn't pleased to see him.

'Has something happened?' she said, hurriedly clamping down on that thought. 'It's not Helen, is it? Nothing's happened to her or the baby?'

'No, they're both fine.' He shrugged. 'I couldn't sleep so I went for a walk. I was just passing and thought I'd check that you were all right after last night's escapade.'

'Oh, I see.' Lucy nodded, although she had no idea why he'd felt it necessary to check on her. 'I'm fine, as you can see, so there's no need to worry about me.'

'Good.' He gave another shrug and she felt a ripple of surprise run through her when she realised how on edge he looked. It was obvious that there was something troubling him and she knew she wouldn't rest until she found out what it was.

'I was about to make some coffee. Would you like a cup?' she offered.

'I don't want to intrude…' he began, but she didn't let him finish. If something was worrying him then she wanted to help, if she could.

'You aren't.'

'In that case, then, thank you. A cup of coffee would be great.'

He stepped into the hall, closing the door behind him. Lucy led the way up the stairs, wondering if she was mad to have suggested it. Getting involved with Max would be a mistake and she knew it, so why was she deliberately courting trouble? She bit her lip as she led him into the flat because ever since she'd met Max she'd been behaving strangely.

'This is…er…cosy.'

Lucy looked round when he spoke, an unwilling smile curling her mouth when she saw him glance around the room. 'That's how the letting agent described it, funnily enough. If you ask me, I think poky sums it up far better.'

Max laughed out loud. 'Now I'm in a real quandary. I don't know whether to agree with you, or be polite and deny it!'

'There's no need to be polite. This place is the pits and anyone can see that. Anyone who's not an estate agent, that is.'

'If it's any consolation it would be classed as spacious in London. Even a broom cupboard down there sends the average estate agent into paroxysms of delight.'

'You lived in London before you moved here?' Lucy asked, making her way to the alcove that served as her kitchen.

'Yes. I went to university in London and ended up staying after I qualified. I lived there for over twelve years, in fact.'

'So why did you decide to leave?' she asked, filling the kettle with water.

'I decided that I wanted a complete change of scene after my divorce.'

'Divorce?' Water slopped onto the work top as she put the kettle down with a thud. 'I had no idea that you'd been married!'

'It's not something I talk about.'

'I understand.' She frowned. 'Although I do find it strange to learn that you were married when you told me quite emphatically that you aren't interested in commitment.'

'I'm not. Let's just say that what happened had a huge bearing on how I view life these days.'

Lucy had no idea what to say to that. However, her heart was heavy as she mopped up the water and plugged in the kettle. Max must have been dreadfully hurt by the failure of his marriage if it had changed his whole outlook on life. The thought of him having loved another woman to such an extent was so painful that she felt tears spring to her eyes and quickly blinked them away. She had no right to feel hurt, no rights at all where he was concerned.

'I imagine we're all influenced by past experiences,' she said quietly, refusing to dwell on that thought.

'We are.' He paused and she heard the question in his voice when he continued. 'I get the feeling that whatever happened in your past has had a big impact on you, too, Lucy.'

Lucy bit her lip as she debated what to say. Should she tell him about Richard and the whole sorry mess? It seemed such a huge step to take and yet she realised all of a sudden that she wanted him to know what had turned her into the person she was today.

'It did. For one thing it led me to move here, and that's something I certainly wouldn't have done.'

'Do you want to talk about it?'

His tone was so gentle that any doubts she had disappeared in a trice. Max obviously cared what had happened to her and the thought made it that much easier to open up.

'There's not a lot to say really. I was engaged to this guy when I discovered that he'd been cheating on me.' She shrugged. 'I'm not the first woman to find herself in that position and I doubt I'll be the last, either.'

'But that doesn't make it any less painful.'

Tears prickled her eyes again when she heard the compassion in his voice. 'No, you're right. It doesn't. I was devastated when I found out what had been going on. It completely knocked my confidence. I thought Richard loved me, you see, but it turned out that he'd been out with a string of women during the time we were together. That would have been bad enough, but what hurt even more was finding out that he'd been seeing my cousin, Amy.'

'That must have been a terrible shock.'

'It was. Our mothers are twins, you see, so Amy and I grew up together. We were always very close but when this came to light, it caused a huge rift not only between us but both our families as well. Mum naturally took my side while my aunt felt she had to defend Amy. It got to the point where they were no longer speaking to each other.'

'It must have been very difficult for you.'

'It was horrible. I felt so stupid too, because it had

never crossed my mind that Richard might be with another woman when he was supposed to be working late!'

Tears began to stream down her cheeks and she heard Max utter a low oath as he pulled her into his arms. 'Don't cry, sweetheart. He isn't worth a single one of your tears after what he did.'

He nestled her head against his shoulder, murmuring softly as all the pent-up emotions came pouring out. Lucy cried until she had no more tears left, but it was the release she'd needed and once it was over, she felt calmer, able to see the situation for what it was. She wasn't responsible for Richard's actions. It had been his choice to cheat on her and she wasn't to blame.

'Are you OK?'

Max's voice was so gentle that she shivered. She felt her breath catch when she looked up and saw the way he was looking at her with such tenderness in his eyes. It seemed like the most natural thing in the world to reach up and press her lips to his…

He uttered something rough deep in his throat as he claimed her mouth in a searing kiss. Lucy clung to him as the room started to spin. When he raised his head and looked into her eyes, she knew that he could see how she felt and didn't care. Maybe it was madness, but at that moment she wanted him to make love to her more than she had wanted anything in her whole life.

CHAPTER TWELVE

Max could feel his heart pounding. There wasn't a doubt in his mind about what he could see in Lucy's eyes, yet how could he respond to it? It wouldn't be right to make love to her when she was so vulnerable.

He gently eased her out of his arms, feeling his heart ache as he was deprived of the warmth and softness of her body. It was a long time since he had denied himself the pleasure of making love to a woman but this wasn't just any woman. This was Lucy and he would do anything to protect her.

'I shouldn't have kissed you like that,' he said gruffly, struggling to come to terms with that idea. What was it about her that made him want to shelter her from harm? He had no idea but he couldn't deny that it was how he felt.

'It wasn't your fault, Max. After all, it was me who started it.'

Max had to steel himself when he heard the plea in her voice. It would take very little to push him over the edge and make him do something he would regret. He had to remember that he needed to protect himself as well as her, and hope that it would help to keep him strong.

'You were upset and I took advantage of that. I'm sorry.' His tone was brusque and he saw her recoil.

'There's no need to apologise,' she replied in a taut little voice that cut him to the quick. 'These things happen so forget it. I'll make us that coffee, or would you prefer tea?'

'Neither, thank you. I think it would be better if I left.' He turned towards the door, pausing when she gave a harsh laugh.

'Don't worry, Max, I'm not trying to trap you, if that's what you're afraid of.'

'Trap me?' he repeated uncertainly, glancing round.

'Hmm. First I lured you up here with the promise of coffee and then I tried to coerce you into my bed with tears.' She stared back at him and his heart ached when he saw the hurt in her eyes. 'You're probably wondering what comes next, so let me make it perfectly clear that I don't expect anything from you. I know you're a free agent and very keen to remain that way.'

'It isn't that.'

'No?'

'No,' he said firmly. He took her hands and held them tightly, wishing he could explain why it would be a mistake for them to get involved. It was only the thought of what she would think of him after he'd told her that stopped him. 'I don't want to hurt you, Lucy. You've had a really rough time recently and you're extremely vulnerable at the moment. It would be only too easy to do something that you'll regret.'

'And you think I'll regret it if we make love?' she said softly, her eyes holding his.

'Yes.' Max had to swallow because his mouth was so dry all of a sudden that it was difficult to speak. 'You aren't the kind of woman who sleeps around,

Lucy. You're the kind who needs commitment and that's something I can't give you.'

He bent and brushed her cheek with his lips, realising his mistake the moment he felt the softness of her skin beneath his mouth. He knew he should pull back but it was impossible to do so when every cell in his body was screaming that it needed this contact, that it needed more...

He turned his head until her mouth was suddenly under his, so soft and sweet, so warm and tempting that he knew he was lost. Hauling her into his arms, he kissed her with all the hunger that had been building up inside him for weeks. That first kiss may have been wonderful but it had barely taken the edge off his desire. He wanted her so much, wanted to kiss her and caress her, wanted to feel her body under his as they reached undreamed-of heights together.

The thought tipped him over the edge. All thoughts of behaving sensibly fled as he trailed kisses along her jaw and down her neck. Her skin was so warm and silky that he groaned as his lips glided over it. When he reached the collar of her robe, he pushed it aside so that his mouth could continue its journey, trailing kisses along her collar bone to the tip of her shoulder before working his way back to the tiny hollow at the base of her throat where a pulse was beating wildly. He paused, feeling the rapid throb against his lips. He had never wanted any woman as much as he wanted her!

'Don't stop.'

Her voice was husky with desire and Max felt every cell in his body react to it. He drew back and looked at her, knowing what he would see in her eyes, yet even then he wasn't prepared for how it made him feel. To know that she wanted him this much was like being offered a slice of heaven.

'I won't stop unless you ask me to,' he told her, his own voice grating with the force of his desire. He knew she understood what he meant when he saw her eyelids lower and tensed. It was one thing to invite his kisses but was she sure that she wanted him to make love to her, one hundred per cent certain that she wouldn't regret it?

Tension thrummed through his body as he waited for her to speak, made him feel so light-headed that it was a moment before he realised that she was looking at him.

'I won't want you to stop, Max. I'm absolutely certain of that.'

It was all he'd needed to hear and his heart leapt with joy as he pulled her back into his arms and held her so that she could feel the power of his arousal pressing against her. When his hands went to the belt on her robe, she trembled, not with fear or uncertainty, he knew, but with a passion equal to his own.

His hands were shaking as he parted the front of her robe because he knew this was a moment he would remember for the rest of his life. He closed his eyes for a second while he savoured the thought then looked at her, letting his gaze travel over the lushly feminine curves of her body. Her breasts were full and beautifully shaped, her waist incredibly narrow, her hips generously curved, and his pounding heart raced out of control.

'You're so beautiful,' he murmured. Reaching out, he let his fingers graze over one taut nipple and heard her gasp, so did it again only it was his turn to gasp this time. Everything about her was perfect, alluring, and he wanted nothing more than to enjoy the delights of her body.

He went to pull her back into his arms but she shook her head. 'No. Not yet. We need to even things up a bit first.'

Max had no idea what she meant and before he could ask, her hands went to the zip down the front of his leather jacket. He hadn't even realised that he was still wearing it until that moment and his head spun when it struck him how completely under her spell he was.

She drew the zipper down and his breath locked in his throat when she slowly parted the edges of his jacket and slid it off his shoulders. It was incredibly erotic to stand there and let her undress him. When her hands went to the hem of his sweater and started to lift it, he felt the blood pound through his veins.

Max stood rigidly still while she drew the sweater over his head and tossed it over the back of the sofa. He could feel the coolness of the air on his bare skin, such a stark contrast to the heat that was building inside him that his desire seemed to double in intensity.

'You're beautiful too,' she whispered huskily. Lifting her hands, she let her palms glide across his chest, a tiny frown creasing her brow as she followed the contours of muscle and bone as though committing them to memory.

Max's stomach muscles clenched when he felt her fingers caressing his skin. Everywhere she touched, nerve endings were firing out signals, alerting him to what was happening. When her palms glided over his nipples, he shuddered as a raft of sensations were unleashed inside him. She must have felt the tremor that passed through him because she paused, her hands resting lightly on his sensitised flesh.

'Did I hurt you?'

'No.' He pulled her back into his arms, feeling his mind explode with desire when her naked body came to rest against his. 'It wasn't pain I was feeling, my sweet. Far from it.'

'Oh!'

Max smiled when he saw her colour. The fact that she could still blush like that when they were on the verge of making love touched him deeply. Bending, he dropped a kiss on her lips then another on the tip of her nose. Her eyelids came next; he kissed her eyes closed, breathing in when he felt her lashes tickle his lips. Kissing had always been a pleasant enough experience in the past, but he had never felt this tenderness before, this desire to protect and cherish. It made him see that making love with Lucy would be unlike anything that had gone before. This would be a first for him in so many different ways.

The thought was just too much. Max kissed her again, on the mouth, with a passion that made them both tremble. He could feel the ripples running under his skin when he took hold of her hand and led her into the bedroom, tiny shock waves of sensation that made his nerves tingle and his flesh feel as though it was on fire. The room was small and cramped even with the bed pushed up against one wall, but he didn't care about their surroundings. He only cared about Lucy and what they were doing.

Sitting down on the bed, he pulled her down beside him and kissed her again, a slow, drugging kiss that soon had them clinging to each other. When she lay back against the pillows and held out her arms, he lay down beside her, smoothing his hand down her body, feeling her skin glide beneath his fingers like warm silk as he followed the curves and dips. They were both breathless when his hand made its way back up and came to rest on her breast, both of them filled with excitement and expectation, and it was the most wonderful feeling to know they were so perfectly in tune.

Max felt joy fill him as he stripped off the rest of his clothes and took her in his arms. This wasn't just sex; it could never be simply that. This was love-making in its purest form, the moment when two people became one single being. As he entered her, he knew that he had been given something so special that he would be forever in her debt. He would never regret this night and he would do everything in his power to make sure that Lucy never regretted it either.

The room was cold when Lucy awoke a short time later. She pulled the covers over her, feeling her heart fill with a host of emotions when her arm brushed against Max's shoulder. She didn't regret what had happened; how could she when it had been so marvellous. However, she knew that it could cause problems in the future. Max had made it clear that this wasn't the start of something more and she mustn't make the mistake of thinking that it was.

'Regrets already?'

She turned when he spoke, seeing the concern in his eyes. 'No. I'm not sorry it happened, Max.'

'But?'

'There isn't a but,' she said firmly, closing her mind to the insidious little voice that was whispering in her ear. She was a grown woman and if they were merely destined to have an affair then she could handle it. She didn't need promises of undying love to make it right! 'I went into this with my eyes open and I don't regret it.'

'Are you sure?'

'Quite sure. How about you, though? Are you sorry it happened?'

'No, I'm not.'

He pulled her to him, his mouth seeking out the hollow at the base of her throat. Lucy shivered when she felt the tip of his tongue tasting her skin. Their love-making had been a revelation. She had never imagined that she could feel such passion. It wasn't just that Max was a skilled lover either; it was the fact that there'd seemed to be a real connection between them. Their minds had been in tune as well as their bodies and it was that which had made it so amazing. If she'd been on the brink of falling in love with him before this had happened, how did she feel now?

Lucy closed her mind to that question because she didn't want to have to deal with the answer. They made love again and it was every bit as wonderful as the first time. As she lay in his arms afterwards, she knew that if there'd been any way to change his mind about the future then she would have leapt at it, but there wasn't. He was determined to stay single and after his previous, unhappy experiences, could she blame him?

The thought that Max must still care for his ex-wife if their divorce continued to affect him nagged away at her as they got up and took a shower. Naturally, they got sidetracked so that it was gone two o'clock by the time they went back into the bedroom. Lucy groaned when she realised how late it was.

'Is that the time already? I'm due in work in a couple of hours.'

'Do you want me to go?' Max offered immediately.

'No!' Lucy flushed when she realised how insistent she sounded. She mustn't make the mistake of appearing needy or she would scare him away. Although she had no idea how long this would last, she wanted to store away enough memories to see her through the coming years.

She gave a light laugh, determined not to look too far into the future. 'You're not leaving until you've had that cup of coffee I promised you. And how about something to eat? My mum would have a fit if she found out that I'd let a visitor leave without offering him sustenance.'

'Mine too,' he agreed, smiling as he fastened the belt on his trousers. 'Sounds as though they'd get on like a house on fire.'

'It does.' Lucy picked up her hairdryer. It was a figure of speech, she told herself sternly. Max certainly hadn't meant to imply that he wanted their parents to meet!

'Shall I make us something while you finish getting dressed?'

Lucy glanced up, feeling her heart turn over when her gaze landed on him. He hadn't put on his sweater yet and the sight of his naked torso made her pulse leap. He looked so wonderfully, gloriously male that it was difficult to concentrate on the question. 'I've not got anything very exciting in the fridge, I'm afraid. It didn't seem worth stocking up on Christmas goodies just for me, so I only bought basics.'

'Leave it to me—I'll see what I can rustle up.'

'Well, if you're sure you don't mind….'

'Of course I don't mind.' He dropped a kiss on her lips. 'You just concentrate on making yourself look beautiful, not that it will take much effort.'

He dropped another kiss on her lips and left. Lucy smiled as she switched on the hairdryer. She hadn't been looking forward to Christmas, but it was turning out to be a lot better than she had expected!

She finished drying her hair then hunted through the wardrobe for something to wear. She finally decided on a pair of black cord jeans teamed with a red velvet top, which looked suitably festive. She could hear Max whistling in the other room and smiled. She definitely hadn't expected to spend Christmas Day with Max either!

As soon as she was ready she made her way into the sitting room, only to come to an abrupt halt at the sight that met her. Max was standing by the stove and he turned when he heard her coming in.

'I hope you don't mind me raiding your cupboards.'

'Of course I don't mind,' she whispered, staring around in amazement.

He had drawn the curtains to block out the daylight and placed lighted candles around the room instead. The soft glow they gave out lent the shabby room an almost magical charm. More candles had been placed in the centre of the table, the flickering light from their flames reflecting off the glasses and cutlery. Lucy was so touched that he had gone to so much trouble that it was several seconds before she could speak.

'I never expected anything like this, Max. It looks absolutely beautiful. Thank you so much for doing all this.'

'So long as you like it, that's all that matters,' he

said softly. He picked up a couple of glasses and came towards her. 'I hope you like Bucks Fizz, although I'm afraid the fizz part is lemonade not champagne!'

Lucy laughed as she accepted one of the glasses. 'I shall make a note to always keep a bottle of champagne in the fridge from now on!'

'Starting with the bottle I owe you.' He gave her a warm smile as he touched his glass to hers. 'Happy Christmas, Lucy.'

'Happy Christmas,' she repeated, feeling a shiver run through her when she saw the way he was looking at her. Maybe it wasn't champagne, but it was every bit as potent as she had imagined it would be to share this drink with him, and the thought made her heart race.

They finished their drinks and Max took the empty glasses over to the sink. He came back and pulled out a chair then bowed. 'If Madame would care to take her seat, luncheon will be served very shortly.'

Lucy giggled as she sat down, loving the fact that he was as happy to play the fool as the ardent lover. 'Thank you, waiter. May I ask what's on the menu?'

'Omelettes *aux herbes fines*. Not exactly Christmas fare, but the chef does make the most amazing omelettes.' He kissed the tips of his fingers and she laughed.

'They had better be good after the build-up you're giving them!'

'Manna from heaven,' he assured her, grinning wickedly as he headed to the stove.

Lucy sighed as she watched him set to work, beating the eggs. It would be only too easy to see this rapport between them as a sign that their relationship would last, but it would be a mistake to do that. She had to remember that Max wasn't interested in her long-term.

It was a sobering thought and one that she couldn't ignore. It was a relief when Max brought in the plates. He set them down with a flourish.

'Luncheon is served.'

Lucy nodded regally, doing her best to play her part. She was going to enjoy this magical Christmas day, every single second of it, and not ruin it by worrying about what might happen in the future. 'Thank you, waiter.'

'My pleasure, Madame.' Tearing off a length of kitchen roll, he draped it across her lap with huge aplomb. *'Bon appétit.'*

'You've obviously done this before,' she said, laughing.

'I have indeed. I waited tables while I was medical school. The extra cash helped to top up my grant. In fact, at one point I was working evenings in a fast food outlet during the week *and* doing silver service in an up-market restaurant at the weekend.'

'Is that where you learned how to make an omelette?' she asked, cutting into her omelette, and he nodded.

'Yep. The chef was a nightmare to work for. He used to throw a tantrum if things weren't done the way he wanted them. Needless to say, the turnover of kitchen staff was horrendous and several times I ended up acting as his sous chef.'

'Really? So how did you get on with him?'

'All right, funnily enough. Oh, he still used to storm around the place but I learned to ignore him. It was good practice for when I did my rotations. Some of the consultants I worked for made him look like a real pussy cat!'

He rolled his eyes as Lucy laughed. She cut another sliver of omelette, sighing appreciatively as she popped it into her mouth. 'This is delicious. How did you manage to make it so light?'

'You add a splash of water to the eggs,' he informed her. 'I've no idea why but it seems to work. And you mustn't beat them too hard either.'

'I'll remember that,' she assured him.

They finished their meal and Lucy made a pot of coffee for them. Max was sitting on the couch when she took the tray in; he looked up and grimaced.

'I'll have dents in my bottom if I sit on this thing for very long. The springs are poking right through the cushions.'

'Tell me about it.' Lucy sighed as she gingerly perched on the edge of the couch and poured coffee into two mugs. 'It should be sent to the tip along with the rest of the furniture.'

'I take it that you rent the place fully furnished?'

'Yes. I couldn't afford to buy furniture when I moved here so I went for the easy option.'

Max frowned. 'I'd have thought it was cheaper living here than in the city. It's definitely less expensive to rent a place, I've found.'

'It is, and once the lease has expired on the flat in Manchester then I'll be much better off. I won't be paying rent on that as well.'

'You're still paying rent on your old flat!' he exclaimed.

'Yes.' Lucy grimaced. 'We'd only just signed the lease when I found out what my ex had been up to. He refused to pay his share of the rent after we split up, so it was down to me.'

'He sounds like a real piece of work,' he said in disgust, then shrugged. 'Sorry. It's not my place to say that.'

Because he didn't want to get involved? Lucy summoned a smile, but it hurt to know that Max was keeping his distance after what they had shared. 'Don't apologise, it's true. I only wish I'd realised sooner what he was like. It would have stopped a lot of people getting hurt.'

'You mean your family? Is that why you decided not to go home for Christmas and New Year, because of the upset it had caused?'

'Yes. I was afraid that if I went home everything would get raked up again and that's the last thing I want.'

'I imagine it would have been difficult to see your cousin after what has happened?'

'It would, although I don't blame Amy. She'd just split up with her boyfriend when Richard came onto her and I think that's why she ended up falling for him. He caught her at a weak moment, not that she was the first by any means.'

Max didn't say anything else. He let the subject drop, not that she was sorry. What had happened suddenly seemed of very little consequence if she was honest. It made her see that her feelings for Richard hadn't been nearly as deep as she'd thought, nowhere near as deep as the feelings she realised she had developed for Max. She knew that when she and Max went their separate ways, it would be far more painful.

CHAPTER THIRTEEN

Max couldn't settle after he left Lucy. He went back home, intending to spend the evening watching the Christmas Day film, but it failed to hold his attention. In the end, he switched off the set while he sat and thought about everything that had happened that day.

Making love to Lucy had been everything he had dreamed it would be and more. He had never expected to feel such a connection to another person as he had felt to her, and the thought filled him with despair because at some point soon he would have to let her go. All he could have were a few short weeks and he really shouldn't allow himself even that much.

He sighed. He had done the one thing he had sworn he wouldn't do and now he had to ensure that he didn't make matters worse. That comment Lucy had made about her fiancé catching her cousin at a particularly vulnerable moment could apply equally to her. It brought it home to him that he needed to be extra-careful about how he handled the situation. Although he wished with all his heart that things could be different, it would be wrong to allow her to fall in love with him. The fact was, she would be much better off without him messing up her life.

* * *

Christmas Day had turned out to be quite busy, Lucy discovered when she arrived for work that night. Cathy was doing the handover and she lost no time updating her.

'There are two mums still in delivery. One's had her baby and she'll be moving onto a ward as soon as Anita has finished tidying her up. The other mum will be a while yet from the look of things. Helen Roberts is in the side room. The diabetes care team have asked us to monitor her blood glucose levels as they've nobody on duty tonight. She's on between-meals testing as well, so the last check will be due around midnight, if you could make a note of that.'

'Of course. What about the baby? How's he doing?'

'Fine. He's feeding well and all the tests are clear.'

'That's good to hear.'

They completed the handover and Cathy stood up to leave. 'That's it, then. Let's hope you have a quiet night, unlike last night.'

'It was quite an experience,' Lucy agreed.

'I'll bet it was.'

There was a strange note in Cathy's voice and Lucy looked at her in surprise. 'Sorry, am I missing something?'

'I heard all about you careering around the country-side with Max. The whole hospital's been buzzing with it, in fact.' Cathy grimaced. 'Tell me to mind my own business, but I think you should know that a lot of folk are wondering if you're the latest candidate to fall under Max's spell.'

'But it was work!' she protested, trying to control the blush that rose to her cheeks. Maybe last night had been to do with work but this afternoon certainly hadn't been.

'That's what I keep telling everyone but you know how people love to gossip, especially about Max. Just be careful, though. I think the world of Max—we all do—but he's an inveterate womaniser. I'd hate you to get hurt, Lucy.'

Cathy said her goodbyes and left before Lucy could say anything. She sighed as she left the office. Whilst she didn't regret what had happened, Cathy's advice was a timely reminder that she needed to take care. Just because she and Max had slept together, it didn't mean they had a future.

The evening flew past. Thankfully, Lucy had no time to brood because she was far too busy. The second baby, a girl, finally made her appearance just before nine p.m. Although it had been a long and tiring labour for the mother, everything was fine. Once mum and babe had been moved onto a ward, Tina went for her break. She'd only just left when the front doorbell rang to warn them there was someone waiting outside. Diane was in the office so Lucy popped her head round the door.

'Someone's just rung the bell. Can you hold the fort while I see who it is?'

Leaving Diane in charge, she hurried downstairs. Security was extremely tight on the maternity unit. All the external doors were kept locked during the night and anyone who wanted to be admitted had to ring the bell. Most mums phoned ahead to warn them they were coming in but there were always a few who just turned up. Opening the door, she peered out but there was nobody about. She frowned, wondering if it had been children playing a trick by ringing the bell. It had happened a couple of times, although it seemed unlikely on Christmas Day. Stepping outside, she scanned the car park but still couldn't see anyone.

Lucy went to go back inside when she heard a noise. She stopped dead, trying to work out where it was coming from. There was a bench seat against the wall close to the door and she realised that the sound was coming from that direction. She hurried over to the bench and gasped when she saw a Moses basket tucked on the end of it. There was a baby in it, wrapped in blankets and with a pale blue knitted hat on its head.

Lucy hurriedly picked up the basket and carried it inside. Although she would have liked to have gone and looked for whoever had left it there, her main concern was to make sure the baby was unharmed. She quickly made her way back to the maternity unit, seeing the shock on Diane's face when she saw what Lucy was carrying.

'Someone left this on the bench by the front door,' she explained as she carried the basket into the office. Placing it on the desk, she stared down at the baby. 'I've no idea who left it there because there was nobody about by the time I got to the door.'

'We'll have to inform the police,' Diane said immediately. 'I'll do it while you make sure he's all right. We'll use one of the delivery rooms for now. There's always a few mums in the nursery at this time of night, doing feeds, and it would be better if we kept this to ourselves for now.'

'Of course.'

Lucy carried the basket into one of the delivery rooms and placed it on the bed. Although the baby was well wrapped up, it was bitterly cold outside and she wanted to make sure that he wasn't suffering from hypothermia.

Babies rapidly lost body heat and even a relatively short period of being exposed to the elements could cause a drop in their temperature. She fetched a thermometer and took his temperature, relieved to find that it was within normal limits. She had just finished when Tina appeared.

'I can't believe this has happened!' Tina exclaimed as she came over to the bed. 'How could any mother abandon her child like that? And on Christmas Day too!'

'Whoever did it must have been desperate,' Lucy said sadly. She lifted the baby out of the basket when he started to grizzle and stroked his cheek. 'He's obviously been well cared for—you can tell that just by looking at him. Both his clothes and the blankets he was wrapped in are spotless.'

'I suppose so,' Tina conceded. 'Anyway, the police are on their way. Diane said to tell you that they want to interview you, apparently. She's going to phone Max and let him know what's happened. I expect he'll be here shortly, too.'

'Oh. Right.' Lucy felt her heart lurch at the thought of seeing Max again so soon. She had to make a conscious effort not to let Tina see how on edge she felt. 'I think this little fellow might be hungry. Will you stay with him while I go and rustle up a bottle?'

Lucy popped the baby back into the basket and made her way to the nursery. There were a few mums in there so she had a quiet word with the sister and explained what had happened. Once she had made up a bottle of milk, she went back to the delivery room. The police had arrived and they were keen to interview her, so she handed the bottle to Tina while she made a statement.

She had just finished when Max arrived and she felt her pulse start to race when he came straight over her.

'Are you all right, Lucy? This must have been a real shock.'

'I'm fine.' She smiled up at him, loving the way his eyes had darkened when he looked at her. Max might be reluctant to commit himself, but he couldn't hide the fact that he cared about her. The thought made her heart overflow with happiness. 'I'm more concerned about finding the baby's mother. She obviously needs help.'

'We'll find her,' he said softly, giving her shoulder a gentle squeeze.

The police wanted to ask him some questions next so Lucy excused herself. Tina had finished giving the baby his bottle so she volunteered to change his nappy. She undid the poppers down the front of his pale blue sleep suit, smiling when he started gurgling and kicking his legs.

'So you think this is a game, do you?' she said, tickling his tummy. He wriggled even harder, his chubby little legs flailing up and down with excitement, and she laughed. 'You're a lively little fellow, I must say.'

She changed his nappy and was about to pop him back into his clothes when Max came over to her. 'The police need his clothes and the basket in case they contain any clues as to who he belongs to.'

'Of course. I'll undress him now.'

Lucy quickly slipped off the baby's sleep suit and vest and handed them to one of the officers who placed them in a plastic bag. Although the mums were asked to bring in clothes for their babies, there was a selection of baby clothes in each delivery room in case someone forgot. She found a fresh vest and a sleep suit and took them over to the bed.

'Can you tell us roughly how old he is, Doctor?' the older police officer asked as Lucy started to dress the baby.

Max frowned. 'Well, he's not a newborn.' He pointed to the baby's tummy. 'The stump of his umbilical cord has fallen off and that usually happens in the first couple of weeks. If I had to make a guess I'd say he's about four to five weeks old and that he's been well looked after too. He's definitely not undernourished.'

'I see. And is there any way of checking if he was born here?' the officer continued, making a note on his pad.

'You think that's why the mother left him here?' Max said in surprise.

'It's possible. Most women who abandon their babies choose a place where they know the child will be looked after. It's possible that this little chap's mum gave birth to him here and that's why she chose to leave him outside your door.'

'It makes sense, I suppose.' Max sighed. 'We keep a record of all the babies who are born in the unit, but I'll need to speak to the hospital's manager before I can give out information like that. It's a question of patient confidentiality, you understand.'

'I understand, Dr Curtis. Rules are rules. But the sooner we find the mother, the better. In my experience, the longer this goes on, the less chance we have of tracing her.'

Lucy could tell that Max was torn between the desire to help all he could and the need to protect their patients' privacy. She hurriedly intervened, wanting to take some of the pressure off him. 'What happens now? To the baby, I mean.'

'He'll be taken into care and placed with foster-parents,' the officer explained. 'I'll get onto the child protection team as soon as we get back to the station and arrange for them to collect him.'

'Actually, I'd feel happier if he remained here tonight,' Max said firmly. 'Although he appears to be perfectly fit and healthy, I'd like to keep him under observation. We can find a place for him in the nursery, can't we, Lucy?'

'Of course,' she said immediately.

The policemen agreed that it was probably the best option and left shortly afterwards to check the CCTV footage. There were cameras covering all the outside doors and they were hoping that the incident had been captured on film. Lucy sighed as she fitted a plastic identification tag around the baby's wrist before she took him to the nursery.

'I hope they find his mother. I hate just putting the date and the time he was found on this tag instead of his name.'

'Hopefully, his mum will come forward soon and claim him,' Max said quietly.

'Is that why you were so keen to keep him here?'

'How did you guess?' He smiled at her. 'I know it's a long shot, but the fact that she left him outside our door suggests that she trusts us. I think it's far more likely that she will get in touch with us if she thinks the baby is here rather than with the police.'

'You could be right. So what do we do if she does contact us?'

'Try to reassure her that she isn't in any kind of

trouble. She must be in a pretty bad state to have abandoned her child like that and the last thing we want is for her to think that she'll be in trouble with the authorities.'

'I feel so sorry for her,' Lucy said sadly, looking down at the baby. 'I can't imagine what she must be going through at the moment, can you?'

'We'll do everything we can to help her, Lucy. I promise you that.'

His tone was so gentle that her heart ached. Max was such a good person, kind, caring, considerate of other people's needs. Maybe he did portray the image of a carefree bachelor, but she was more convinced than ever that it was all a front. It didn't seem right that he should continue to deny himself the kind of life he deserved because his first marriage had failed and she needed to make him understand that.

'Look, Max,' she began, then stopped when the door opened and Diane appeared.

'Sorry, Max, but you're wanted on the phone. It's Alan Harper, the hospital's manager. Apparently, the press have found out about the baby being abandoned and phoned him at home.' Diane grimaced. 'He's none too pleased, either, seeing as he knew nothing about it.'

'How on earth did they get hold of the story so soon?' Max exclaimed, hurrying to the door. He paused to glance back. 'Can you book him into the nursery and make sure all the staff know that any phone calls concerning him are to be directed to me. There'll probably be a lot of crank calls once the news gets out, but if the mother does phone, I want to speak to her.'

'I'll make sure everyone knows what to do,' she assured him, and he smiled.

'Thanks, Lucy.'

Lucy sighed as she took a blanket off the rack and wrapped the baby in it. Maybe it was a good thing that she'd been interrupted when she had. It wasn't her place to give Max advice and he would probably have resented her interfering. After all, if he'd wanted to change the way he lived, he would have done so. The fact that he hadn't pointed to just one thing: he must still be in love with his ex-wife if their divorce continued to exert such an influence over him.

She knew she should accept that, but it was hard to accept that Max loved another woman after what they had shared that afternoon. She had felt closer to him that day than she'd felt to anyone else and knew that if she continued to see him, her feelings would grow stronger. She knew that she should call a halt but she couldn't face the thought. The truth was that she had fallen in love with Max and didn't want to lose him.

By the time Max returned to the maternity unit, over an hour had passed. Alan Harper had decided to consult a member of the trust's legal team to ask his advice about handing over the information the police had requested. He'd insisted that Max should be included in the discussion so a conference call was set up. However, in the end nothing definite was decided. It seemed that everyone was reluctant to take any steps that could result in the trust being sued, so more lawyers would need to be consulted before a final decision was made.

Max was seething when he stepped out of the lift. Although he understood the need to protect their patients' privacy, nobody seemed to appreciate how urgent the situation was. Lucy was working at the desk and she frowned when she saw his grim expression.

'What's wrong?'

'Bureaucracy gone mad is what's wrong. Instead of doing all we can to help the police find the mother, we've been banned from handing over any information.' He shook his head. 'Everyone's more concerned about the trust being sued than anything else.'

'It's a sign of the times,' she said softly. 'Court cases are rife these days. Nobody's immune, not even hospitals.'

Max sighed. 'You're right, of course. It's just so frustrating not to be able to do anything to help.'

'I know.' She picked up a printed sheet and handed it to him. 'I checked back through our files and this is a list of all the babies born here during the past six weeks. If we discount all the girls it leaves fifteen in total.'

Max glanced at the paper and shook his head. 'Nothing leaps out at me. How about you?'

'I feel the same. I recognised some of the names, the babies I delivered, but that's as far as it goes. He could be any one of them.'

'Or he might not be on this list at all. After all, there's no guarantee the baby you found was born here.'

'That's what's so worrying. The police have so little to go on.'

'Did they find anything on the CCTV footage?'

'Yes, but it's not much help, I'm afraid.'

She handed him half a dozen grainy photographs. Max grimaced as he squinted at the blurred image of a hooded figure carrying the Moses basket. 'You can't even tell if it's a man or a woman from these!'

'I know. The police have taken the tape back to the station to see if they can clean it up, but they didn't sound too hopeful. In the meantime, they want us to show these pictures to everyone who works here in case someone knows who it is.'

'I doubt they'll recognise her from these.' He handed back the photographs. 'There's been no phone call?'

'Not yet, but everyone knows what to do if she rings,' she assured him.

'There's not much more we can do, then, is there?' He glanced at his watch and groaned. 'It's gone midnight already!'

'I didn't realise it was so late. I need to check Helen Roberts's blood glucose levels again.'

She got up and came around the desk. Max stepped aside to let her pass, feeling his body stir when she accidentally brushed against him. He took a deep breath to control the surge of desire that flooded through him, but he could tell that she'd realised what was happening when he saw her face colour. It took every scrap of willpower he possessed not to haul her into his arms and kiss her until they were both senseless.

'I'll be in the office if you need me,' he told her, his voice grating from the strain of keeping a rein on his feelings.

'You're not going home?' she asked, and he could hear the tension in her voice too. His heart started to race when he realised that she felt exactly the same as he did.

'No. I'd rather stay here in case the mother phones.'

'She might not phone tonight, though. It could be to-morrow before she plucks up enough courage, or the day after that. You can't work twenty-four hours a day, Max, until she gets in touch. You'll wear yourself out!'

Max smiled when he heard the concern in her voice. It felt good to know that she cared about him, very good indeed. 'I understand that, but if she does call tonight then I'd like to be here so I can talk to her.'

'It's up to you, of course. But promise me that you'll be sensible and go home in the morning.'

'I promise, on one condition.'

'And that is?'

'That you'll come home with me, Lucy.'

CHAPTER FOURTEEN

PALE winter sunshine was filtering into the room when Lucy awoke. Just for a second she had no idea where she was before it all came rushing back. She was in Max's flat. In his bed.

Rolling onto her side, she studied his sleeping face as she recalled what had happened when they had arrived at his apartment earlier that morning. Their hunger for each other had been so great that they hadn't made it further than the living room. Max had made love to her right there on the sofa, his powerful body pressing her down into the smooth leather cushions. It had been an explosion of raw passion, the release they had both needed so desperately. Max had wanted her as much as she had wanted him; surely that had to mean something?

Lucy sighed as she tossed back the quilt. Maybe he *did* want her but it wasn't proof that he was looking for more than a physical relationship, was it? She had to accept that this was probably all she could have and enjoy it while it lasted.

She made her way into the en suite bathroom and stepped into the shower. Like the rest of the apartment, it was state of the art and she spent several minutes trying to work out how to turn on the water. She was so engrossed that when the glass door slid back and Max appeared, she jumped.

'I wondered where you'd got to.'

'I…um…I was attempting to take a shower,' she explained, feeling her breath catch when he stepped into the stall. Even though it was only hours since they'd made love, she could feel the hunger building inside her again as she took stock of his naked body.

'It can be a bit tricky to work out all these switches,' he agreed, reaching past her to turn one of the dials. Water suddenly began to flow from the shower head and she gasped when she felt its coolness on her bare skin.

'It's freezing!' she protested, trying to move out of the way.

He caught her hand and stopped her. 'You won't feel cold in a moment,' he said softly, his eyes holding hers as he raised her hand to his lips.

Lucy's pulse leapt when she felt his tongue glide across her palm. When he reached her wrist he didn't stop but carried on up the inside of her arm, licking the droplets of moisture off her skin. Although the water was still beating down on her, she no longer felt cold but boiling hot, burning up inside. When his mouth moved from her arm to her breast, she cried out, shuddering as his lips closed over her nipple. Her legs felt so weak all of a sudden that she could barely stand but he eased her back against the tiles and held her there while his lips and tongue continued to work their magic, licking, stroking and caressing every inch of her until she was mindless with passion.

He drew back and looked into her eyes. 'Do you still feel cold?'

'No,' she murmured, feeling herself trembling with desire.

'Good.'

He smiled as he lifted her until she was straddling his hips. His mouth found hers at the very moment that he entered her and she closed her eyes as a wave of intense pleasure swept through her. She didn't need to look at Max to know that he felt the same. They were so completely in tune that she could tell exactly how he was feeling. She clung to him as they climaxed together, and in the final second, just before the world dissolved, she couldn't hold back any longer.

'I love you,' she whispered. 'I love you.'

Max could feel the words echoing inside his head, growing louder and louder with every beat of his heart. Lucy loved him—could it be true?

He wanted to leap up and punch the air in delight, but how could he? How could he celebrate when it was the one thing he should never have allowed to happen?

He set her back on her feet, reaching around her to turn off the water, feeling the pain bite deep into his gut when he saw her eyes open because he knew he would have to hurt her.

'Max? What is it? What's wrong?'

He had to steel himself when he heard the alarm in her voice. It would be so easy to accept what she was offering him, but it wouldn't be right when he had nothing to offer her in return. 'We need to talk, Lucy.' Opening the glass screen, he took a towel off the rack and handed it to her. 'Why don't you get dressed while I make us some coffee?'

'I don't want coffee! I want to know what's wrong.'

'Let's leave it until we're dressed,' he said flatly, deliberately removing any trace of emotion from his voice.

She didn't say another word as he stepped out of the stall, but she didn't need to. Max could feel her pain as he strode into the bedroom and dragged on his clothes. He didn't think he had ever felt as bad as he did at that moment, knowing that he had to hurt her even more. It was only the thought that he was doing it for her sake as well as his that gave him the strength to continue.

The coffee was ready by the time she appeared at the kitchen door. Max filled a couple of mugs and placed them on the table then pulled out a chair for her, but she made no attempt to sit down. She just stood and watched him, her face looking unnaturally pale in the glare from the overhead spotlights.

'So this is it, Max? You've had enough of me already?'

Her tone was bitter and he flinched. Sitting down at the table, he took a sip of his coffee, hoping it would steady him. He needed to make her understand that this was the right decision, the *only* decision that made any sense.

'I told you that I wasn't looking for commitment,' he said quietly.

'Yes, you did. No one could ever accuse you of being untruthful.' She laughed, and his heart ached when he heard the pain in her voice. 'I suppose it's my own fault. I committed the ultimate sin, didn't I? I should never have told you that I loved you.'

'Look, Lucy…'

'No. Please don't say anything. I feel foolish enough without you trying to reassure me that it doesn't matter. All I can say is that I'm sorry if I embarrassed you, Max. I never intended to do that.'

She spun round on her heel and he realised that she was going to leave. Was that what he really wanted? Did he want her to walk out of his life, thinking that she'd been at fault in some way? He shot to his feet and hurried after her. She already had her coat on by the time he reached the sitting room and his hands clenched when he saw her fumble with the buttons. He couldn't bear to know that she was upset and that it was all his doing.

'Lucy, I'm sorry! If anyone's to blame then it's me. I should never have got involved with you in the first place. I knew how dangerous it was but I kept telling myself that I could handle it.'

'Dangerous,' she repeated, turning to look at him. 'What do you mean by that?'

'That I knew from the first moment we met that I could very easily fall in love you.'

'And would that have been such a bad thing?' she asked, her voice catching.

'Yes.' Max could feel the blood pounding through his veins. He knew there was only one way to make her understand why they couldn't have a future and that was to tell her the truth. The thought of how she would react was almost more than he could bear but he had to do it.

'I'm no use to you, Lucy. ' He held up his hand when she went to interrupt. 'No, let me finish. The fact is, I'm no use to any woman because I can never father a child.

That's why you're better off without me messing up your life.'

Lucy felt the room start to spin. She grabbed hold of a chair and clung to it while everything whirled out of control. She heard Max say something but she had no idea what it was. When he took her arm and sat her down on the sofa, she didn't protest. She couldn't. Every single word seemed to have disappeared from her mind apart from the words he had uttered: he could never father a child.

'Here, drink this.'

He placed his mug of coffee in her hand and helped her raise it to her mouth. Lucy shuddered when she felt the hot liquid trickle down her throat. She took another sip then set the mug down on the coffee table, afraid that she might drop it. Max was sitting beside her now and she could tell that he was waiting for her to speak, but what could she say? She was so shocked by what he had told her that she had no idea how to respond.

'Wh-when did you find out? That you couldn't have children, I mean?' she managed at last.

'Three years ago. Becky and I had been trying for a baby for a while. When nothing happened, we decided to have some tests done.' He shrugged. 'It turned out that I was to blame.'

'It must have been a terrible shock for you,' she said softly.

'It was.' He gave her a tight smile and her heart wept when she saw the anguish in his eyes. 'I've always loved kids and just assumed I'd have some of my own one day. Finding out that the chances of it happening were virtually nil was a lot to take in.'

'But there is still a chance that you could father a child,' she said quickly.

'A very *slim* one. Apparently, I produce enough sperm but they have poor motility.'

'Surely there are steps you could have taken? I don't know much about fertility treatment but they can do wonderful things these days. Did you and your wife never think of trying it?'

'No. To be honest, I don't think we could have coped with the strain, let alone the disappointment if it had failed. We'd been going through a rocky patch even before we decided to try for a baby and that was the final straw. It was simpler to call it a day.'

'I'm so sorry, Max. It must have been a horribly difficult time for you.' She squeezed his hand, wishing there was something she could say to make him feel better.

'It's all over and done with now.'

He moved his hand away, making it clear that he didn't want her sympathy, and she sighed. Although she understood how painful it must have been for him to discover that he was unlikely to father a child, he couldn't let it affect his life for ever.

'Are you sure about that?'

'What do you mean?'

'You already admitted that your divorce is the reason why you steer clear of long-term relationships. It doesn't sound to me as though it's all over and done with from that.'

'Obviously, it has a bearing on how I lead my life these days. It wouldn't be right for me to expect any woman to forgo having children because of me.' He looked steadily back at her. 'I certainly wouldn't put you in that position, Lucy. It wouldn't be fair.'

'But surely it should be my choice,' she protested.

'Some choice.' His tone was grim. 'Stick with me and give up your dreams of becoming a mother. Or find some other guy who can give you all the children you want. I know which option I'd choose.'

'You make it sound so…so *clinical*! But you can't just turn your feelings on and off like a tap, Max.'

'You can when it's the sensible thing to do.' He stood up abruptly. 'Maybe you think you could live with the situation right now, but a few years down the line, you'll change your mind.'

'How do you know that?'

'Because I've seen how you are with the babies on the ward, how much you love them. Be honest, Lucy. Do you really think that you'll be happy if you never became a mother? Because I don't.'

Lucy hesitated. Although she longed to deny what he said, it wouldn't be right to do so without thinking about it first. She had always assumed that she would have a family one day, so could she really imagine being childless?

'I thought not.' Max obviously took her hesitation as a sign that she agreed with him. His face was set when he looked at her. 'I don't think there's any point letting this affair continue, is there?'

'If it's not what you want, Max, then, no, there isn't any point.' She stood up, trying not to let him see how much it hurt to hear him speak to her in that distant tone. Tears stung her eyes as she picked up her bag. It had never been just an affair to her. It had been so much more!

'You may as well know that I'm planning on leaving Dalverston in the near future. That should make life simpler for you.'

Lucy couldn't hide her surprise as she turned to him. 'Leaving?'

'Yes.' He shrugged. 'I decided that it was time I applied for a permanent consultant's post. Anna is due back from maternity leave at the end of January so it's the perfect time to make the move. I have a couple of interviews lined up in the next few weeks, so hopefully it won't take too long to find a suitable position.'

'Then all I can do is wish you luck,' she said hollowly, her head reeling when it struck her that he must have been planning his departure for some time if he already had interviews scheduled. The thought that she had only ever been a fleeting distraction to him was more than she could bear and she knew that she had to leave before she did the unforgivable and broke down.

She hurried to the door and let herself out, bitterly aware that Max didn't try to stop her. Why would he when he was probably relieved to see the back of her? All that talk about him being afraid of falling in love with her had been so much hot air. There'd never been any chance of that happening!

Tears ran unchecked down her face as she hurried down the drive. She'd thought she knew how it felt to have her heart broken but she'd been wrong. This was far worse than anything she had experienced before. She had lost the man she loved with all her heart and she couldn't imagine how she would ever get over it.

Max stood at the window, watching as Lucy ran down the drive. The urge to go after her and beg her to forgive him was so strong that he almost gave into it. His hands clenched as he fought for control but it was hard to stand there and watch her walking away from him. Maybe he had done the right thing, the *only* thing, yet he couldn't help feeling as though he had thrown away something really precious. There was going to be a huge gap in his life now that Lucy would no longer be a part of it.

The days passed in a blur. Lucy was aware that she was functioning on autopilot most of the time but it was the only way she could cope. If she allowed herself to think about what had happened then she would break down.

Thankfully, she saw nothing of Max. Although she knew he was in work during the day, he was never around when she arrived in the evening for the night shift. She suspected that he was avoiding her and was relieved. The less she saw of him the better, she told herself, but it was hard to pretend that everything would be fine when it was such a long way from being that.

Fortunately, they continued to be extremely busy and that helped. The baby she had found had been placed with foster-parents now. The mother still hadn't contacted either them or the police. Although permission had been granted to hand over the details of all the babies born in the unit during the period in question, nothing had turned up during the police's enquiries. Lucy knew that any hopes of tracing the mother were fading fast.

Her second stint of nights came to an end on New Year's Day and she had the rest of the week off. She was planning to go home and visit her parents. What had happened in the past had paled into insignificance compared to recent events and it was time her family knew that she had put it behind her. She was planning to catch the ten o'clock train because as she knew from experience, it was pointless trying to sleep when she got in. As soon as she closed her eyes, her mind started racing, going over everything Max had said to her. She had to accept that whatever they'd had was over.

Lucy made herself a cup of tea when she got home then took a shower. It was barely eight o'clock by the time she got dressed again, way too early to set off to the station. She decided to go to the newsagent's and buy a magazine to read on the journey, so fetched her coat. It was still very cold outside but the snow had disappeared at last. After she'd bought her magazine, there was still plenty of time left before she needed to leave so she decided to go for a walk. The canal was close by and a walk along the towpath would help to blow away some of the cobwebs.

There were a couple of people walking their dogs along the path when she set off but apart from them there was nobody about. She decided to walk as far as the lock and then make her way back. She could see the old lock-keeper's cottage in the distance and guessed it would take her about ten minutes to get there. She rounded the final bend and stopped when she saw a familiar figure standing on the edge of the lock basin. It was Sophie Jones, the young mum whose baby she had delivered on her first day at Dalverston General. She couldn't imagine what Sophie was doing there at that hour of the day and hurried towards her.

'Sophie? Are you all right?'

Sophie spun round and Lucy tried to hide her dismay when she saw the state the girl was in. Her clothes were filthy and it looked as though she hadn't washed in days.

There was no sign of Alfie and Lucy's heart turned over as she wondered what had happened to him.

'What are you doing here, Sophie?'

'Nothing. I...I just felt like a walk, that's all,' Sophie muttered.

'Me too. It's a lovely morning, isn't it?' She gave the girl a reassuring smile. 'Where's Alfie? Have you left him with someone, a friend or a neighbour perhaps?'

'I don't know where he is, but he's better off without me!'

Tears suddenly began to pour down Sophie's face, and Lucy felt more alarmed than ever. 'What do you mean that you don't know where Alfie is? What have you done with him?'

'I left him outside the hospital,' Sophie whispered. 'I knew he'd be safe there.'

'Alfie was the baby I found on Christmas Day!' Lucy exclaimed in shock.

'Yes.' Sophie gulped. 'I didn't know what else to do. I tried phoning everyone I could think of—the clinic, the doctor, the health visitor—but all I kept getting were messages to say that I should call back after Christmas. I couldn't wait that long. Not with the flat in that state!'

'Tell me what happened,' she said firmly. 'Why was your flat in such a state?'

'It was some boys. They broke into the flat above mine and ripped out all the pipes. There was water pouring through my ceiling, so I got in touch with the landlord, but he wasn't interested when I told him what had happened. He's planning to sell the building to a property developer and he couldn't care less what goes on there. Most of the other tenants have moved out because they couldn't put up with the conditions any longer.'

'It sounds dreadful.'

'It is. I put out pans and bowls to catch the water, but on Christmas Day the whole ceiling fell in. Everything was ruined—the furniture, Alfie's pram, every single thing I own.'

'I am so sorry, Sophie. I can't imagine how you must have felt. Is that why you left Alfie at the hospital?'

'Yes.' Sophie dashed her hand across her eyes. 'I didn't want to do it, but how could I keep him when we had nowhere to live? I thought he'd be better off with someone else, someone who could look after him properly.'

She gave a choked little sob as she turned away. Lucy wasn't sure what happened next, whether she lost her footing or deliberately stepped off the lock wall, but one minute Sophie was standing in front of her and the next second, she had disappeared.

'Sophie!'

Horrified, Lucy ran to the lock and peered into the water, but there was no sign of the girl. Instinct kicked in at that point, cutting through her panic. Shrugging off her coat, she leapt into the lock, gasping when the icy water closed over her head. Kicking her feet, she propelled herself back to the surface and looked frantically around. Sophie was floating, face down, on the water a couple of yards away so she swam over to her. She managed to roll her over and was relieved when the girl started to cough.

'You'll have to help me,' she panted, struggling to keep them both afloat. The water was so cold that her legs were already going numb and she knew that she wouldn't be able to support them for very long. 'Try to kick your feet while I tow you over to the side.'

Sophie did as she'd instructed but it was obvious the cold was affecting her too. It seemed to take for ever to reach the side of the lock where metal rungs had been embedded in the wall to form a ladder. Taking hold of the girl's hand, Lucy closed her fingers around one of the rungs.

'Do you think you can climb up?' she panted, her breath coming in laboured spurts.

'I...don't...know,' Sophie replied, her teeth chattering with cold.

'You have to try. Come on. I'll help you.'

She managed to guide Sophie's foot onto a rung then used her shoulder to boost her up the ladder. It was painfully slow and Lucy could feel her hands as well as her legs going numb with the cold. Sophie was halfway up the ladder now and she knew it was time that she got out as well.

She grabbed hold of a rung and tried to haul herself out of the water, but the weight of her clothing was dragging her down. It didn't help either that her hands were so cold that it was hard to maintain her grip on the metal rung.

Lucy gasped as she fell back into the water. She could hear Sophie shouting and did her best to reach the ladder, but she was too far away from it now. The water closed over her head as she sank beneath the surface and her last thought before the blackness descended was about Max and how much she loved him. It didn't matter if they could never have a family; she just wanted to be with him.

CHAPTER FIFTEEN

IT WAS the worst week of Max's entire life. Worse even than when he'd found out that he would never be a father. He missed Lucy so much, missed seeing her smile, hearing her laugh, just missed being with her. In the short time he had known her, she had come to mean the world to him and he couldn't imagine what his life would be like without her. It was only the thought of the harm it could cause that stopped him seeking her out and telling her how he felt.

He spent New Year's Eve at home on his own, having turned down several invitations. He didn't feel like celebrating and would have been very poor company if he'd gone out. He went into work on New Year's Day and did his best to appear upbeat when everyone wished him a happy new year but his heart was heavy. He wasn't looking forward to the coming year when he would be leaving Dalverston, and leaving Lucy.

He tried to shrug off the feeling of hopelessness and concentrated on work. There'd been two admissions during the night and both mums were hoping that their baby would be the first to be born in the unit that year. One of the women had suffered from high blood pressure throughout her pregnancy and when her BP started to rise to dangerous levels, Max decided that a section would be the safest option.

The procedure went smoothly and he was back on the unit within the hour. Amanda was on the phone when he returned and he could tell that she was upset. 'What's happened?' he asked as soon as she'd hung up.

'That was A and E on the phone. Apparently, they've got Lucy down there. I'm not sure what's happened exactly, but they said something about her being pulled out of the canal.'

'The canal!' Max exclaimed in horror. 'Did they say anything else, has she been badly injured?'

'No. They just asked if we had a contact number for her family. I said I'd have a look and phone them back.'

'I see.' Max spun round, his heart hammering with fear. The situation must be serious if A and E needed to get in touch with her family. 'I'm going down there right now. Page me but only if it's urgent, OK?'

'I…um…yes, of course,' Amanda agreed, looking a little startled by his hasty departure.

Quite frankly, Max didn't care what anyone thought. His only concern at that moment was Lucy and what had happened to her. He ran along the corridor, taking the stairs two at a time rather than waiting for the lift. A and E was heaving with people but he pushed his way through the crowd gathered around the Reception desk.

'You've got Lucy Harris here. Where is she?' he demanded when the receptionist looked up.

'I'm not sure. Just let me check.' The woman started to scroll through a list of names on her computer while

Max tried to curb his impatience. 'Ah, yes, here it is. She's in Resus, Dr Curtis.'

'Thanks.'

Max hurriedly made his way along the corridor, feeling his stomach churning as he stopped outside the door to Resus. This was where the most seriously injured patients were treated and he couldn't bear to think that Lucy was in need of this kind of specialist care. His hand was shaking as he pushed open the door because he didn't know what he would do if anything happened to her.

'Max! This is a surprise. What are you doing here?'

Max looked round when he recognised Sam Kearney's voice. 'I believe you've got Lucy Harris in here. How is she?'

'A lot better than she was, I'm happy to say.'

Sam led him over to the corner and pushed aside a screen. Max felt his heart bunch up inside him when he saw Lucy lying on the bed. She was covered from toes to chin with insulated blankets and there was another blanket wrapped around her head. Although her eyes were closed he could hear her breathing and some of his panic subsided. She was alive and that was the most important thing.

He turned to Sam. 'Do you know what happened? Someone said that she'd been pulled out of the canal.'

'That's right. From what I can gather, she jumped in to rescue a girl who'd fallen into the lock. Lucy managed to help her out but couldn't get out herself. It was pure luck that a chap walking his dog heard the girl screaming for help. He managed to haul Lucy out.'

'Thank heavens for that!' Max declared in relief. 'So how badly injured is she?'

'She's suffering from hypothermia. Core body temperature was a shade below thirty-five degrees when she was admitted but, as you can see, it's risen since then.' Sam directed his attention to the monitor and Max nodded.

'That's a positive sign, isn't it?'

'It is, although she's not out of the woods just yet,' Sam warned him. 'As the body's temperature drops, there is increasing dysfunction of all the major organs, so we'll need to monitor her for the next twenty-four hours or so. On the plus side, however, her heart rate is steady and her sats are improving.'

'I see.' Max went over to the bed, feeling his heart swell with relief when Lucy's eyes slowly opened. 'How do you feel?' he asked, his voice thickened with emotion.

'I'm not sure. Cold, I suppose. And scared...'

She tailed off as though it was too much effort to continue. Max reached for her hand and held it tightly in his. 'There's nothing to be scared about, sweetheart. I'm here now and I'm going to take care of you, if you'll let me.'

Bending, he pressed a gentle kiss to her lips, feeling his pulse leap when he felt her kiss him back. In that moment everything became crystal clear. He loved her and that was why he'd been so scared when he'd found out she'd been injured. He had been fighting his feelings for weeks but he could no longer hide from the truth. He loved her. It was as simple and as complicated as that. He was still reeling from the discovery when he heard Sam laugh.

'Ever had the feeling that you're surplus to requirements? I'll be back in a few minutes, not that I think you're going to miss me.' Sam looked pointedly at the ceiling. 'Whoever put that there has a lot to answer for.'

Max grinned when he saw the bunch of mistletoe hanging from the ceiling. 'Remind me to thank them!'

Lucy smiled as Sam sketched them a wave and left. 'If you're not careful, people will start talking. You don't want to ruin your reputation, do you, Max?'

'For being the eternal bachelor, you mean?' He raised her hand to his lips. 'Those days are well and truly over.'

'Are they?' she whispered, searching his face.

'Yes.' He took a deep breath. It was such a huge step and he wasn't sure even now if it was the right thing to do.

'Just tell me, Max.'

Her voice was soft, the look she gave him so filled with love that all his doubts disappeared. Bending, he looked into her eyes, wanting there to be no mistake about what he was saying. 'I love you, Lucy. I love you with all my heart and my soul and I want to spend the rest of my life with you, if you'll let me.'

She closed her eyes for a moment and when she looked at him again he could see tears sparkling on her lashes. 'I love you too, Max. With my heart and my soul and every tiny bit of me.'

'Oh, my darling!' He swept her into his arms and kissed her with all the love he felt. He had never dreamt this moment would happen so it made it all the sweeter, all the more precious. They were both breathless when he let her go and he laughed wryly as he checked the monitoring equipment.

'Hmm, your pulse rate shows a definite increase and your temperature has risen too. This could be an alternative method for treating cases of hypothermia. What do you think?'

'Fine, so long as it's only me you're planning on treating, Dr Curtis.'

Max chuckled. 'Oh, it is. Most definitely.' He kissed her lingeringly then smiled into her eyes. 'I'm not interested in anyone else. I haven't been interested since I met you.'

'No?' She arched a brow. 'What about that date you had a couple of weeks ago?'

'A complete and total failure. I spent the evening wishing I was with you,' he confessed.

'So it didn't lead to a night of unbridled passion?' she asked lightly, but he heard the question in her voice.

'No, it didn't. You stole my heart the moment I met you, Lucy. It just took me a while to admit it. But you're the only woman I want, now and for evermore.'

'I'm so glad,' she said simply. 'It's how I feel too. You are the only man I shall ever want.'

'You do understand what it means, though, about us not having a family,' he said quietly, because he needed to be sure that she had thought it through properly.

'Yes. I wish things could be different, Max, but I know that I'll be happy so long as I have you.'

'Are you sure? It's such a big decision and I don't want you to regret it at some point.'

'I won't regret it. I promise you that.' She smiled up at him with her heart in her eyes. 'I love you, Max, and whatever the future brings, we shall face it together.'

Max was so choked with emotion that he couldn't say anything. He kissed her on the mouth, letting his lips say everything he couldn't. There were tears in his eyes this time when he drew back. 'I love you, Lucy. I want to spend my life with you so will you marry me? Please.'

'If you're sure it's what you want then yes. Yes, I'll marry you, Max!'

Max gave a great whoop of joy. He was about to take her back in his arms when he suddenly became aware that people were clapping. He pushed back the screen, grinning when he discovered that they had attracted an audience. 'I take it that you lot were listening?'

'Too right we were.' Sam clapped him on the shoulder. 'It's not every day that you get to hear the hospital's most die-hard bachelor being brought to heel!'

Everyone laughed at that, Max included. He turned to Lucy and smiled. 'I hope you weren't planning on keeping this a secret.'

'No. I don't care who knows.'

'Let's hope you still feel that way after the hospital grapevine gets to work.'

He pointedly closed the screen then kissed her again. One kiss led to another and probably would have led to many more if his pager hadn't bleeped. He groaned as he unhooked it off his belt and checked the display. 'Maternity. I hate leaving you here like this, but I have to go. I'll come back as soon as I can—that's a promise.'

'I understand, Max, and I'll be fine, honestly.' She kissed him on the mouth then sighed. 'Odd how something so wonderful has come out of what could have been a tragedy.'

'It is. Sam told me that you saved someone's life,' Max said soberly. 'You were very brave, Lucy.'

'I only did what anyone else would have done.' She

frowned. 'Did you know that it was Sophie Jones who fell into the lock?'

'No, I had no idea! What was she doing by the canal in the first place?'

'I'm not sure, but she was in a terrible state. It will take too long to explain it all to you now, but that baby I found was hers. It was Alfie.'

'Really?'

'Yes. I'll tell you the whole story later when you've got time to listen. All I will say is that I can understand why she left him outside our door. That poor girl has been through an awful lot and she desperately needs help.'

'Then we'll make sure she gets it.'

He gave her a last kiss then made his way back to the maternity unit. It was obvious from the expressions on people's faces that the hospital grapevine had already been working overtime but Max didn't care who knew about him and Lucy. In fact, he was sorely tempted to take out an advert in the paper and announce the news to the world at large. The woman he loved had agreed to marry him. Now, that really was a cause for celebration!

Christmas Day, one year later...

Lucy smiled as she walked into the sitting room and knelt down in front of the Christmas tree. Although it was ridiculously early, she hadn't been able to stay in bed any longer. Excitement coursed through as she placed a small package under the tree. It might not look very much but she knew that Max would love this gift more than any other.

'So this is where you've got to.'

She looked round when Max suddenly appeared, feeling her heart fill with love. The past year had been so wonderful that several times she'd had to pinch herself to prove she wasn't dreaming. They had been married in the spring in a simple civil ceremony held in the grounds of a hotel on the banks of Lake Windermere. Her cousin Amy had been one of her bridesmaids, along with her sister and Max's three small nieces. Family was important to them both and it was good to know that any rifts had been healed.

They had stayed in Dalverston after both agreeing that they wanted to start their married life there. Max had been appointed to the post of consultant on a permanent basis when Anna Kearney had decided not to return to work following her maternity leave. Although they both lived and worked together, Lucy knew that she would never grow tired of being with Max. He was her whole world.

'I couldn't sleep,' she told him as he came and crouched down beside her.

'Too excited about what Santa has brought you, I expect,' he said, dropping a kiss on her lips.

Lucy sighed as she snuggled against him. She had never realised how much she could love someone until she had met him. 'I love you,' she murmured.

'And I love you too.' He kissed her again then picked up one of the gaily wrapped parcels. 'Happy Christmas, my darling.'

Lucy took it from him and ripped open the paper. There was a velvet-covered box inside and she gasped when she opened the lid and saw a silver charm bracelet

nestled against the satin lining. 'It's beautiful, Max! I
love it.'

'Good.' He took the bracelet out of its box and fastened it around her wrist. 'The woman in the jeweller's
shop told me that it holds about twenty charms, so that's
the next twenty Christmases covered. I thought I'd start
you off with this.'

He showed her the first charm, a tiny silver elephant,
and she laughed. 'A reminder of our honeymoon in
Thailand? We had such fun that day when we rode those
elephants, didn't we?'

'We did, but then every day I spend with you is fun,
Lucy.' His eyes were tender as they traced her face and
she sighed.

'We're so lucky, Max. We have everything anyone
could want.'

'Yes, we do,' he agreed, but she saw the cloud that
crossed his face and knew what he was thinking.
Happiness bubbled up inside her as she thought about
the gift she had placed under the tree. She was going to
save it till last because she knew that Max was going to
love it more than any other.

They took it in turn to open their presents, eagerly
exclaiming at what the other had bought for them. By
the time they finished there were just a few gifts left
under the tree. Max picked up a large box covered in
red paper with tiny reindeer printed all over it.

'Alfie is going to love this. I can't wait to see his face
when he sees this toy tractor.'

'I think you like it almost as much as Alfie will,'
Lucy teased, laughing at him.

True to his word, Max had done everything in his
power to help Sophie. He had contacted the local council

and insisted that she should be placed on their priority housing list. Sophie had moved into her new flat in the summer and was thrilled to have a place of her own. He had also liaised with the child protection team and it was thanks to Max that Alfie was now back home with his mother and obviously thriving. The fact that Sophie was planning to train as a nursery nurse was yet more proof of how the girl had turned her life around with a bit of help.

'What's this?' Max frowned as he held up the parcel she had placed under the tree that morning. 'I don't remember seeing this before. Who's it for?'

'You,' Lucy said simply.

'Me?' He ripped off the paper and Lucy saw the colour drain from his face as he stared down at the plastic wand it had contained. 'Is this what I think it is?' he said, his deep voice grating.

'Yes.' Reaching over she pointed to a small window in the plastic stick. 'See those two blue lines? They mean I'm pregnant. Happy Christmas, Max. You're going to be a daddy.'

'But how…? When…?'

Words failed him and she laughed because she knew exactly how he felt. She felt that way too, stunned and gloriously, wonderfully happy.

'I think *how* it happened is pretty easy to explain. We just did what any couple does when they love each other. As for when—well, by my reckoning it must have been that weekend we spent in Paris. The dates certainly fit. According to this, I'm eight weeks pregnant.'

'I can't believe it.' There were tears in his eyes as he reached out and pulled her into his arms. 'I know that doctor I saw didn't completely rule out the chance of it happening, but I thought he was trying to let me down gently.'

'Apparently not.' She kissed him on the mouth, then drew back and looked at him. 'I know it must be a shock for you…'

'It is! But it's the most wonderful shock I've ever had. Thank you, Lucy. Thank you so much. Sharing my life with you has been like a dream come true and to know that we're having a baby as well is just the icing on the cake. I didn't know it was possible to feel this happy!'

He kissed her hungrily, telling her through actions as well as words how thrilled he was. Lucy kissed him back, feeling her heart swell with joy when she realised that this time next year they'd be parents. They would be celebrating Christmas as a family and she couldn't wait!

ST PIRAN'S: ITALIAN SURGEON, FORBIDDEN BRIDE
by Margaret McDonagh

Talented neurosurgeon Gio Corezzi's deliciously dark good looks turn the heads of every female at St Piran's Hospital—except quiet beauty Jess Carmichael. As she and her bundle of kittens are about to be homeless for a while, Gio has his chance to rescue them both and claim the vulnerable Jess's heart!

THE BABY WHO STOLE THE DOCTOR'S HEART
by Dianne Drake

Dr Mark Anderson's work in White Elk is definitely temporary— there'll be no looking back. Except he meets beautiful single mum Angela and her adorable baby girl and, by the time he has to leave, he's desperately looking for a permanent role—as part of their little family.

**On sale from 7th January 2011
Don't miss out!**

Available at WHSmith, Tesco, ASDA, Eason and all good bookshops
www.millsandboon.co.uk

★ ★

are proud to present our...

Book of the Month

St Piran's: Penhally's Wedding of the Year & St Piran's: Rescued Pregnant Cinderella

from Mills & Boon® Medical™ Romance 2-in-1

ST PIRAN'S: THE WEDDING OF THE YEAR
by Caroline Anderson
GP Nick Tremayne and midwife Kate Althorp have an
unfulfilled love that's lasted a lifetime. Now, with their
little boy fighting for his life in St Piran's Hospital...can
they find their way back to one another?

ST PIRAN'S: RESCUING PREGNANT CINDERELLA
by Carol Marinelli
Dr Izzy Bailey is single and pregnant when she meets
the gorgeous neo-natal nurse Diego Ramirez. When
she goes into labour dangerously early Diego is there to
rescue her... Could this be the start of her fairytale?

Available 3rd December

Something to say about our Book of the Month?
Tell us what you think!

millsandboon.co.uk/community
facebook.com/romancehq
twitter.com/millsandboonuk

A Christmas bride for the cowboy

Two classic love stories by bestselling author
Diana Palmer in one Christmas collection!

Featuring

Sutton's Way
and
Coltrain's Proposal

Available 3rd December 2010

"Did you say I won almost two million dollars?"

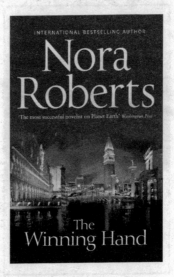

INTERNATIONAL BESTSELLING AUTHOR

Nora Roberts

'The most successful novelist on Planet Earth' *Washington Post*

THE Winning Hand

Down to her last ten dollars in a Las Vegas casino, Darcy Wallace gambled and won!

Suddenly the small-town girl was big news— and needing protection. Robert MacGregor Blade, the casino owner, was determined to make sure Darcy could enjoy her good fortune. But Darcy knew what she wanted; Mac himself. Surely her luck was in?

Available 3rd December 2010

www.millsandboon.co.uk

2 FREE BOOKS
AND A SURPRISE GIFT

We would like to take this opportunity to thank you for reading this Mills & Boon® book by offering you the chance to take TWO more specially selected books from the Medical™ series absolutely FREE! We're also making this offer to introduce you to the benefits of the Mills & Boon® Book Club™—

- **FREE home delivery**
- **FREE gifts and competitions**
- **FREE monthly Newsletter**
- **Exclusive Mills & Boon Book Club offers**
- **Books available before they're in the shops**

Accepting these FREE books and gift places you under no obligation to buy, you may cancel at any time, even after receiving your free books. Simply complete your details below and return the entire page to the address below. You don't even need a stamp!

YES Please send me 2 free Medical books and a surprise gift. I understand that unless you hear from me, I will receive 5 superb new stories every month including two 2-in-1 books priced at £5.30 each and a single book priced at £3.30, postage and packing free. I am under no obligation to purchase any books and may cancel my subscription at any time. The free books and gift will be mine to keep in any case.

Ms/Mrs/Miss/Mr _____ Initials _____

_____

Surname _____

Address _____

_____

_____ Postcode _____

E-mail _____

Send this whole page to: Mills & Boon Book Club, Free Book Offer, FREEPOST NAT 10298, Richmond, TW9 1BR.